Welcome back to Penhally Bay!

Mills & Boon® Medical™ Romance welcomes you back to the picturesque town of Penhally, nestled on the rugged Cornish coast! With sandy beaches and breathtaking landscapes Penhally is a warm, bustling community, cared for by the Penhally Bay Surgery team, led by the distinguished and commanding Dr Nick Tremayne.

So turn the page and meet them for yourself…

And if you've never visited Penhally before, step right in.

WITHDRAWN

Dear Reader

I was overjoyed to be asked to write one of four new books that follow on from the original *Brides of Penhally Bay* series. The opportunity to go back to Cornwall and catch up with the characters who brought the first series to life was too good to be missed.

Penhally is a special place, where hearts are made whole. GPs Luca d'Azzaro and Polly Carrick are two people urgently in need of some Penhally magic to help them recover from tragic events in their pasts.

For Polly, returning to the village where she grew up knowing only unhappiness and neglect takes courage. She faces a difficult journey if she is to lay ghosts old and new to rest, opening her mind and her heart to the possibility of a happy future.

For Luca, moving to Penhally marks the start of a new chapter in his life—and that of his young twins. A devoted father, Luca will make any sacrifice necessary to ensure the welfare of his children, even if it means putting his life and happiness on hold. In Penhally, meeting Polly, will he begin to live again and find that he can have it all?

At the end of Series One we asked, 'Is this the end? Or is it just the end of the beginning?' Bringing these four new books to a close, I can ask the same question! Again, some threads are left hanging, in the hope that we can return to Penhally in the future, to meet new friends and to continue the lives of the special people who live, work and love in this beautiful part of Cornwall.

Happy reading

Margaret

www.margaretmcdonagh.com

A MOTHER
FOR THE
ITALIAN'S TWINS

BY
MARGARET McDONAGH

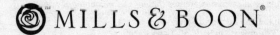

First published in Great Britain 2009
Paperback edition 2010
Harlequin Mills & Boon Limited,
Eton House, 18-24 Paradise Road, Richmond, Surrey TW9 1SR

© Harlequin Books S.A. 2009

Special thanks and acknowledgement are given to Margaret McDonagh for her contribution to the *Brides of Penhally Bay* series.

ISBN: 978 0 263 86987 3

Harlequin Mills & Boon policy is to use papers that are natural, renewable and recyclable products and made from wood grown in sustainable forests. The logging and manufacturing process conform to the legal environmental regulations of the country of origin.

Printed and bound in Spain
by Litografia Rosés, S.A., Barcelona

Margaret McDonagh says of herself: 'I began losing myself in the magical world of books from a very young age, and I always knew that I had to write, pursuing the dream for over twenty years, often with cussed stubbornness in the face of rejection letters! Despite having numerous romance novellas, short stories and serials published, the news that my first "proper book" had been accepted by Harlequin Mills & Boon for their Medical™ romance line brought indescribable joy! Having a passion for learning makes researching an involving pleasure, and I love developing new characters, getting to know them, setting them challenges to overcome. The hardest part is saying goodbye to them, because they become so real to me. And I always fall in love with my heroes! Writing and reading books, keeping in touch with friends, watching sport and meeting the demands of my four-legged companions keeps me well occupied. I hope you enjoy reading this book as much as I loved writing it.'

www.margaretmcdonagh.com
margaret.mcdonagh@yahoo.co.uk

Recent titles by the same author:

ITALIAN DOCTOR, DREAM PROPOSAL
THE REBEL SURGEON'S PROPOSAL
THE EMERGENCY DOCTOR CLAIMS HIS WIFE
DR DEVEREUX'S PROPOSAL*

*Brides of Penhally Bay

With special thanks to:

Sheila, Lucy and the Meds team,
for inviting me back to Penhally.

Jo, my very special editor,
for her patience, kindness and support.
I couldn't do this without you.

Caroline, Christina, Pam and Maggie,
for the gift of friendship
and for seeing me through
some difficult times.

CHAPTER ONE

'GOOD morning, everyone. If I could have your attention.'

As Dr Nick Tremayne strode into the staffroom at the Penhally Bay Surgery on a sunny Monday morning in mid-September, GP Polly Carrick slipped unnoticed to a chair and sat down. Although it was two hours until her first scheduled appointment, Polly had come in early for the meeting, hoping to use the extra time to make an impression on the mountain of paperwork growing on her desk.

'Could we move along, please?' The bite of impatience in Nick's voice was symbolic of the edgy, unpredictable mood he had been in during the last few weeks. 'Patients will soon be arriving—and I have an upcoming meeting. Before then, I have a couple of items to discuss with you.'

The senior partner, Nick's restlessness was evident as he waited for the room to quieten and the on-duty staff to settle. Finally, a hush descended, broken only by the clink of tea-spoons against mugs and the familiar metallic ping as the tin containing practice manager Hazel's home-made biscuits was opened with customary eagerness.

'The last couple of years have brought many changes, not only to Penhally in general but to this practice in particular as we continue to expand and extend the services offered to patients.' Nick paused, an aloof smile on his face as his dark gaze scanned the room. 'Luca d'Azzaro is joining us today, filling the gap created by Adam's departure two weeks ago. Some of you met Luca during his familiarisation visit in August, but for those of you not yet acquainted, he moved to Cornwall from Italy three years ago, working since then in St Piran.'

A frown of consideration knotted Nick's brow. 'I won't be betraying any confidences when I tell you that Luca's ambition was to be a paediatric surgeon, but a change in circumstances led to him switching specialty and qualifying as a GP. His references are exceptional and, having done surgical and trauma rotations during his training, he will be an asset in our minor injuries unit. I trust you'll all extend a warm welcome and offer any assistance Luca needs.'

Murmurs of agreement rippled around the staffroom, which was situated on the first floor of the ever-growing and increasingly busy Penhally Bay Surgery. Polly tuned out Nick's voice as he moved on to the next item on his agenda. Luca's arrival meant that *she* was no longer the newest member of the team. She'd joined the practice nine weeks ago and had settled well, enjoying the job and receiving a warm welcome from the rest of the staff.

Settling in Penhally itself had presented a bigger challenge. She was no stranger to the north Cornish village, having spent the first seventeen years of her life here. Most of them had been unhappy, tormented years. At least, after her mother had died when Polly had been four, leaving her alone in the charge of Reg…a man singularly unsuited to the role of father. A shiver ran down her spine. Polly wrapped her arms around her waist, as if by doing so she could protect herself from the remembered pain. This was neither the time nor the place to poke around in old wounds.

News of the new GP post in Penhally had come out of the

blue. When Kate Althorp—godmother, friend, confidante, and the only person with whom she had kept in touch after leaving Cornwall thirteen years ago—had phoned, Polly had thought she was joking.

'I know how difficult the last few years have been, Polly, and I'm so proud of you for overcoming yet another ordeal,' Kate had told her, bringing a lump to Polly's throat. 'In your last email, you said you needed a complete change and wanted to get right away from London.'

'Yes, I did. I do. But *Penhally*?'

'I know, my love, but all the bad you once knew here has long gone. I've recommended you to the team and told them about your professional skills. There will be an interview, of course, but that's just a formality. The job is yours…if you want it,' her friend had continued, countering her protests. 'Starting over is never easy, as you know from past experience, but here you have people waiting to welcome you back with open arms. And I'm at the head of the queue.'

The lump in her throat had swelled to mammoth proportions. 'Kate…'

'*Please* come, Polly. You're a wonderful doctor. Penhally needs you. And I think you need Penhally. Don't let the shadows of the past continue to cloud your future,' Kate had advised, genuine emotion in her voice.

Although doubts and anxieties had remained, Polly had gone through the interview, agreed terms and signed a contract. Which was why, thirteen years after she had left, vowing never to set foot in the village again, she had found herself back in Penhally.

The meagre possessions she had salvaged—all she had left to show for her years of independence and her folly—looked lost in the Bridge Street flat where Nick's daughter Lucy had once lived and which was now rented out. Kate, ever thoughtful, had stocked the flat with basic supplies and fresh flowers for her arrival.

'Polly?'

Nick's impatient voice, accompanied by a gentle nudge from Chloe Fawkner, who had come to sit next to her, roused Polly from her introspection. She looked up, uncomfortably aware that she had no idea what her boss had said. Everyone was looking at her and a blush heated her cheeks…she hated being the centre of attention.

Trying not to squirm, Polly met her boss's enigmatic gaze, hoping she didn't look as flustered as she felt. 'Yes, Nick?'

'Thank you, Polly. I'm glad you agree,' he replied, turning away.

Amusement rippled round the room and, with a sinking heart Polly wondered what she had unwittingly agreed to. Chloe sent her a sympathetic smile. Besides Kate, it had been Chloe, physiotherapist Lauren Nightingale and their partners who had gone out of their way to include her, both professionally and socially. It was the social stuff she struggled with.

Polly remembered Chloe and Lauren from school. And Sam Cavendish, a part-time GP in the practice, had been in her year. Not that he would have noticed her. No one had. She'd been the quiet, skinny loner who'd lurked in the background.

In the weeks since she had returned to Penhally, Polly had come to know Chloe as a dedicated professional, very caring of her mums-to-be, kind to her colleagues and a good friend to Kate. Chloe had matured into a beautiful woman, with long, dark hair and big green eyes. Polly couldn't help but envy her looks and curvy body. Or the fact that Chloe was so evidently in love with, and loved by, her wickedly handsome husband, Oliver Fawkner, another of Penhally's GPs.

With Nick busy talking to Croatian GP Dragan Lovak,

Polly quizzed Chloe on the details she had missed from their boss's talk.

'What have I agreed to do?' Polly whispered.

Chloe leaned closer to murmur her reply. 'Babysit our new doctor.'

'Oh, hell.'

Polly slumped back on her chair and stifled a groan. It was the last task she would have chosen. Surely one of the more established doctors would be better suited for the role? Oliver had been Polly's mentor for the first few days. He'd been kindness itself, warm in his welcome, and whether or not he had sensed her nervousness, Oliver's easygoing nature and irreverent humour had set her at ease. The least she could do was extend the same courtesy to Luca, although her shyness and anxiety would make her task harder. With patients, she was fine, able to project her work persona, but she continued to find any kind of social interaction difficult.

The morning briefing came to an end, and the staffroom emptied as everyone dispersed to their own rooms and designated tasks. There was no opportunity to talk to Nick. Used to keeping in the background rather than pushing herself forward, by the time Polly had urged herself to act it was too late, and her boss was already out of the door.

'I'll bring Luca along and introduce you in time for your first consultation, Polly,' he called over his shoulder, before jogging down the stairs.

Sighing, Polly found herself alone in the staffroom. After making a mug of white tea with cranberries, she went downstairs to her consulting room and closed the door, determined to do battle with the never-ending paperwork.

As she settled at her desk and sipped her tea, her mind drifted to the new doctor and the little Nick had said about him. She couldn't help but wonder what had caused Luca d'Azzaro to give up his surgical career and why he had turned to general practice instead. Polly shook her head. Such speculation was pointless. And Luca's decisions were none of her business.

Polly glanced at her watch and a frission rippled down her spine, a curious flicker of…what? Apprehension, unease, excitement? She didn't know. She'd never experienced such nervy anticipation before. Why now? And why had Nick chosen *her* to help Luca settle in? All too soon she would meet the mysterious new doctor for herself.

'I think that covers everything, Luca.' With a benevolent smile, Nick leaned back in his chair and closed the file he'd had open in front of him. 'Do you have any questions?'

Luca shook his head. 'No, thank you. I'm eager to begin my new duties.'

Eager, yes, but he also felt a flicker of nervousness at what lay ahead, Luca acknowledged, facing his first day in his first full-time position as a general practitioner. As a young medical student he'd been determined to turn his dream of being a paediatric surgeon into a reality, but fate had had other plans for him, and he'd learned some valuable, if painful lessons. In consequence, he was here today, a qualified GP, embarking on a new chapter of his life.

He'd got just far enough in his surgical training to have had a tantalising taste of what he'd longed for before it had been taken away again. But when life dealt a cruelly vicious blow, a man had to make sacrifices and carry on as best he could. The change of career allowed him more settled working hours so that he could be a better father to his fast-growing twin daughters. And no sacrifice was too much, no cost too high for him to pay, in an attempt to compensate his girls for the fact that they didn't have a mother. The familiar sting of pain, betrayal and crushing burden of guilt weighed heavily upon him.

'We're delighted to have you on board,' Nick said, rising to his feet.

Luca stood up and shook the older man's hand. 'Thank you.'

Nick gestured for him to precede him to the door. 'I've arranged for you to shadow Dr Polly Carrick. You can sit in on her surgeries today, before starting your own consultations tomorrow, and you can double up on home visits for a couple of weeks to learn your way around.'

Luca murmured his acquiescence. It was what he'd expected, Nick having raised the issue when Luca had last visited the surgery to formalise his appointment. He'd looked round the premises on that occasion and had been very impressed by the expansion and all the new facilities. He'd also met some of his soon-to-be colleagues, all of whom had been friendly and welcoming. Their reaction, and the feeling of ease he had experienced being in the surgery, had given him confidence that he'd made the right decision to pursue the sought-after position in Penhally.

He'd yet to meet Polly Carrick, however, and wondered why Nick had chosen her as the doctor he was to shadow.

'Polly joined us in July. She grew up in Penhally, so is familiar with the district.'

'I'm sure her local knowledge will be useful,' Luca responded politely.

Turning down a corridor that housed the physiotherapy room and three consulting rooms, Nick opened an unmarked door and showed him inside. 'This will be your domain. Say if there is anything that you need. You have your name-plate?'

'Yes.' Luca sneaked a quick look around as he moved to set his bag on the empty desk. The room was bright and airy, quite big enough and very well equipped. He opened the bag and took out the plate. 'Here it is.'

Nick smiled. 'You do the honours.'

As he slotted the plate bearing his name into the empty bracket on the door, Luca experienced a sense of achievement and belonging tinged with sadness.

'Next to you is Gabriel Devereux,' Nick informed, pointing towards the door. 'I think you met him the last time you were here.'

Luca smiled, remembering the warmth of the French GP's greeting. 'Yes, I did. And his fiancée, Lauren.'

'Of course. That's Lauren's domain,' Nick told him, gesturing to the physiotherapy room across the other side of the wide corridor. 'And here we have Polly.' His new boss halted outside the closed door bearing her name. 'I've paired you with Polly for several reasons. One was your desire to see your girls settled at nursery school before you came in—and Polly's first appointment on a Monday is at ten o'clock, whereas the other surgeries have been under way for an hour or more.'

Luca was relieved and grateful that the initial understanding Nick had shown was being maintained. 'I appreciate your thoughtfulness. It's true that I wanted time to see them settled on their first day, but I don't expect any undue concessions… and I fully intend to pull my weight on the team.'

'I never expected any different, Luca,' the older man reassured him. 'As the father of twins myself—who are now grown up with children of their own—I can only imagine how difficult it is and what commitment you show in bringing them up alone.'

'Thank you, Nick.'

The words had touched him. But Luca wondered how understanding his new boss would have been had the girls succeeded in scuppering his efforts to get them organised and had made him late on his first day of work. This was a new move and a new routine for them to get used to, and he was well aware that, at three years of age, the twins were also facing challenges in their lives.

He had dropped them off for their first day at nursery. Christine Galloway, the owner of the highly respected school, and Trish Atkins, who taught the three-year-old reception class, had assured him that Rosie and Toni would be fine. Luca smiled. He was more worried what mischief the twins might get up to!

Both girls had been keen to go and make new friends. Even so, he'd had a lump in his throat the size of a boulder when he had left them half an hour ago. It wasn't the first time they had been parted, of course. The twins had been looked after by their grandparents so he could work, first at St Piran Hospital to finish his rotations and then as he'd done his general practice training. But this was their first day at proper nursery school and marked a big stepping-stone in their lives. All three of them were facing changes…a new home, a new school for the girls, and a new job for him.

Nick knocked on Polly's door and a female response from within invited them to enter. Luca felt a strange prickling along his nerve-endings as he heard the voice, which was soft and throaty yet undeniably feminine. Trying to shake off the odd sensation, he followed Nick into the room, completely un-prepared for the slam of awareness that crashed into him when he closed the door, turned round and looked at Polly Carrick for the first time.

Having felt nothing at all for a long time, the immediate, instinctive and unwanted reactions unnerved him. He took an involuntary pace backwards, one part of his brain screaming a denial, while the other part drank in every detail, trying to hang onto each rapid-fire sensation and observation.

The first inescapable truth was that Polly was tiny. It wasn't that she was particularly short—as she stood up, Luca judged her to be around five feet four or five—but even wearing what looked like several layers of colourful but shape-hiding clothes, there hardly seemed to be anything of her at all. And she looked so *young*, scarcely more than a child herself.

The fine features of her face highlighted her delicate bone structure…accentuated further by the way she had swept soft, wavy strands of ash-blonde hair up into a loose knot at the back of her head. A few strands had escaped to feather her face and her slender neck, and his fingers itched to feel their texture and to tuck them back behind her neat, shell-like ears. The fine line of her jaw held a touch of stubbornness in the set of her chin, as if she had been forced many times to punch above her weight in order to be taken seriously. She had high cheekbones and a small, straight nose, baby-soft, pale skin, and a mouth that screamed temptation, the unglossed lips plump and rosy, designed for kissing, and settled now in a natural, sexy pout.

Then he looked at her eyes… Luca sucked in a ragged breath. Polly Carrick had the most beautiful eyes he'd ever seen. Fringed by ridiculously long sooty lashes, they were like the finest sapphires, a rich, deep blue with a luminous effervescence shining within them. They widened now as her gaze met his, and the predominant emotions he saw were confusion, awareness and a touch of fright.

'Luca, meet Polly. Polly, this is Luca d'Azzaro,' Nick introduced them, apparently oblivious to the charge of…what?

Dio! What on was going on here? Whatever it was, Polly didn't want it any more than he did and was fighting just as hard to deny it. Luca tried to gather himself, but it proved impossible to ignore the zing of electricity that awakened every cell in his body as, unable to avoid it, he shook Polly's reluctantly offered hand.

'How do you do?' she greeted him, her words polite but shaky, her voice having the same effect on him now as when he had first heard it from the other side of the door. 'Welcome to Penhally.'

He was acutely aware of her hand in his, of the delicate bones he feared would snap if he held her too tightly and of the brush of her satin-soft skin. Looking down, he saw her paler flesh offset against the darker tones of his, and her whole small hand disappeared, enveloped within his.

'Thank you, Polly.'

Somehow he managed to force the words out. Seconds ticked by, then Polly was drawing away, gently tugging on the hand he still held within his own. Shocked at his uncharacteristic behaviour, Luca abruptly let her go. How was he going to cope being in her company for a day, let alone the two weeks Nick had decreed?

'Polly, I was telling Luca why I've paired you together even though you've not been with us very long yourself,' Nick explained, continuing to show no sign that he had noted the heightened atmosphere in the room. 'One reason is your remarkable affinity with troubled youngsters, hence the drop-in clinic I encouraged you to set up.'

Luca glanced at Polly, noting at once how uncomfortable she was. Nick's 'encouragement' might well come across quite differently if you were on the receiving end and brought in against your will to carry out one of his ideas.

'It wasn't my intention to work with a specific age group,' Polly began, her puzzlement evident.

'However it came about, you're doing an excellent job and we want to give you all the support we can.' With a benevolent smile, Nick continued, 'The Saturday drop-in clinic has been up and running for about a month now, and it's open to all those under eighteen who may not usually consider consulting a doctor. They can come informally for help and advice about anything that is bothering them.'

'It's an excellent idea,' Luca agreed, impressed that Polly had apparently got the whole thing going single-handedly.

'Knowing of your own interest in paediatrics, especially the older age range, I thought the project would interest you. You'll bring Luca up to date on things, won't you, Polly?'

'Of course, Nick.'

Luca met her gaze and noted her reluctance. His interest was piqued by the clinic…and by Polly. He could shout denials from the rooftops, but Polly, with her beautiful eyes and elfin face, dressed in her gypsy-like clothes and fizzing with barely suppressed energy, had made a startling impression on him.

'Good, good,' Nick said, rubbing his hands together. 'Luca, I'll leave you to decide if you want to be involved and can volunteer any hours to Polly—but only if it fits in with your other commitments.'

By which Nick meant the twins, Luca knew. 'Thank you.'

He had a way out and could say no from the outset, removing himself from the possibility of spending even more time around Polly. He opened his mouth to do just that, but before he knew what he was doing or could listen to the voice of reason nagging at the back of his mind, his words emerged very differently.

'I'm sure Polly and I can arrange something.'

'Splendid. And that reminds me,' Nick continued, turning to Polly with an apologetic smile, 'John Whittford, headmaster at the high school, received the flier you sent out about the drop-in service and he's very keen to give it his backing.'

Polly's smile lit up her face and took Luca's breath away. 'I'll contact him and discuss it,' she said, sitting down again and pulling her diary towards her.

'Ah…' Nick grimaced, a guilty expression in his eyes.

'Is there a problem?' she queried, glancing up, even white teeth nibbling the luscious swell of her lower lip.

Luca smothered a groan as he watched her, feeling the

ache tighten deep inside him in response to the sensual gesture. He was relieved when Nick began speaking again, and he struggled to focus on the conversation and not on watching the only woman to have captured his attention and imagination in the last four years.

'I somewhat jumped the gun,' Nick confessed, his arms folded defensively across his chest. 'John requested that you visit the school one day this week to speak to the pupils at assembly about the new service and I pencilled you in for Friday. Luca can go with you.'

'I see.'

Nick seemed unaware of Polly's reaction to his words but Luca, who had been watching her, despite his determination to do otherwise, had seen the flicker of distress in her eyes and had noted that she had visibly paled, her hands clenching until her knuckles turned white. He wondered what was wrong. Was she upset that Nick had committed her to something without her knowledge and agreement? Or was the cause something much deeper? He didn't know, but he intended to find out—on Friday, if not before.

'Right, I think that's all. Luca, let me know if there is anything you need.' Nick shook his hand once more, then turned to Polly with a nod and a smile before glancing at his watch. 'It's almost ten. I'll leave you both to your morning surgery—and to get to know each other. I'm sure you'll work well together.'

The words hung in the air as Nick crossed to the door and let himself out. A tense, charged silence remained, shimmering between them. Luca had no idea how well he and Polly would work together. What he did know was that neither of them relished the situation in which they now found themselves. Perversely, that only intrigued him more and made him wonder what Polly's reasons were for keeping her distance and ignoring the connection they had both felt from the moment they had looked at each other. They might both resist it, but that didn't make it any less real. Or go away.

Meeting Polly's sapphire-blue gaze and seeing the turbulent emotions in the depths of her eyes, Luca had no doubt that getting to know each other was going to be a challenging experience, one that neither of them had anticipated or wanted—but one which was now unstoppable and that neither of them would forget.

CHAPTER TWO

HER immediate and uncharacteristic response to Luca d'Azzaro was a temporary aberration, Polly reassured herself. These peculiar feelings would pass. They had to. Any moment now she would be able to breathe again. Her heart would return to its normal, regular rhythm rather than beating out a manic tattoo like a jungle drum sending an SOS message. The restriction in her throat would ease, the aching knot deep inside her would unravel, her skin would stop tingling and her braless breasts would no longer feel so sensitised that even the soft cotton material of her crop top felt too much against taut, peaked nipples.

She took a hasty, surreptitious glance down at herself, thankful that her propensity for wearing several layers of loose clothing to disguise her body meant that the betraying evidence of her arousal to Luca was not obvious for all—and especially the man himself—to see.

'Would you like a cup of coffee or anything?' she asked, wishing that her voice sounded less breathy and more controlled as she broke the tense silence. She glanced at her watch. 'There's just time before the first appointment.'

'No, thank you, Polly. I'm fine.'

Fine... Not the word most people would use to describe this man. An inch or two shy of six feet, and dressed in a perfectly tailored dark grey suit with a white shirt and a dark purple tie, he was, quite simply, the most stunningly gorgeous man she had ever seen. Around her own age of thirty, she estimated, his hair was short, thick and lustrous, and so dark it was almost black. The strongly defined angles of his face and clean-shaven jaw screamed masculinity. His mouth, with the sensual fullness of his lower lip and the attractive bow of the top one, promised sinful pleasure, while his eyes, under the neat dark slashes of his brows and framed by long, thick, dusky lashes, were the colour of rich, dark melted chocolate. They were deep and mysterious, burning with suppressed passion, and as she looked into them, Polly felt as if she was slipping away from reality.

And, as if his looks and sheer presence were not enough to bring her to her knees, there was his voice. Deep, warm and smoky. He spoke fluent English, but the lilting Italian accent added an undeniable sexiness and every word vibrated along her nerves.

When they had shaken hands, Polly had been struck by the stark contrasts between them. The darker tones of his olive-hued skin had highlighted the paleness of her own, as well as making her hand seem impossibly small and fragile as it all but disappeared within the clasp of his. It had made her feel both vulnerable yet protected. And given the very real sense of danger that had overwhelmed her the instant their gazes had met, she was confused how she could, at the same time, feel so safe.

Polly was shocked by Luca's effect on her, and the magnetic pull she felt. Attempting to cover her nervousness, desperate to focus on something else, and wishing for her world to be normal again, she turned away and busied herself making extra space on her desk. She then fetched a chair for Luca so he could observe the computer screen.

'Thank you,' she murmured as Luca took the chair from her and eased it into place. 'Did Nick tell you about the shadowing?'

'I was expecting it, yes.'

'As well as doubling up for a couple of weeks on home visits to become familiar with the district, Nick likes new doctors to spend the first day learning the way things are done in the practice in terms of sending off blood tests and samples, processing notes, referral letters, prescriptions and so on before taking their own consultations,' she told him, aware she was babbling but unable to stop herself.

Luca's sudden smile—revealing a dimple in his left cheek and laughter lines bracketing his eyes—took away any remaining breath she had left. 'It makes sense. Left to my own devices I could well crash the system on my first day!'

His wry laughter and self-deprecating humour were unexpected and infectious, and Polly found herself smiling back, liking him far more than she wanted to. Once more her gaze clashed with his and a tingle shimmied down her spine. The connection between them was undeniable, the awareness indisputable…and she was scared. She didn't want to like him or be attracted to him.

She'd fallen for a handsome face once before, and look how that had turned out. Polly had learned the lessons of the last painful years. The hard way. And she wasn't about to repeat her mistakes. It didn't matter how incredible Luca was…she had vowed never to get involved with a man again and she had no intention of changing her mind or of opening herself up to any more heartache. She'd do well to remember that, she warned herself, making a supreme effort and dragging her gaze free of his.

'If you're ready, Luca, we should make a start.' Taking her place at her desk, she pulled the tray of notes towards her. 'We have a full list before lunch, then several home visits this af-

ternoon before the next scheduled surgery, which begins at
four o'clock.'

'I'm ready, Polly.'

How could such innocuous words make her pulse race and
her chest feel tight? It hadn't been the words themselves but
the delivery of them…that rough baritone voice could make
a shopping list sound sexy. Polly sucked in a steadying breath
as Luca drew up his chair and sat down. He was far, far too
close. Now, every time she needed to use the keyboard, she
would have to lean into Luca.

Gritting her teeth, Polly tried to keep as much distance
between them as possible as she reached across for her mouse.
Being right-handed, she kept it on the right side of her keyboard,
an added disadvantage now, but Luca picked it up and teased
the cable through so she could use it without stretching.

'Thank you,' she murmured, flicking a sidelong glance
towards him and finding him watching her.

Discomfited, she concentrated with more care than necessary
on opening the required program, checking her morning list
before accessing the first patient's record and giving Luca a
quick briefing. He leaned forward to study the notes and was so
close that Polly became aware of his scent. She couldn't put a
name to it but, whatever it was, the subtle, faintly musky aroma
was so incredibly sexy that it inflamed her senses and made her
want to burrow into him and absorb the very essence of him.

Aware her eyes were closing and she was in danger of
swaying towards him, just as instinct demanded, Polly jerked
backwards, hastily fumbling with the first packet of notes she
had drawn from the box. She cursed herself, feeling her
cheeks warm with embarrassment. What was wrong with her?
She never reacted like this, yet a few moments in Luca's
company and she was thinking and feeling uncharacteristic
things. Thank goodness she only had to do consultations with

him for one day. Even so, she wasn't sure she would survive it. She didn't want to think about two weeks trapped in the car doing home visits with him.

Her hand was shaking as she reached for the phone to buzz Reception. She hoped Luca hadn't noticed—or, if he had, that he had no idea being in close proximity to *him* was the cause.

'Hello, Sue,' she said when the head receptionist answered the phone. 'We're ready to start. Could you send the first patient through, please?'

'Of course, Polly.'

Polly hung up the phone, surprised when she heard Luca sigh and whisper a couple of words in Italian. She didn't understand what he'd said, but she caught the sentiment.

'Nervous?' she asked, her gaze drawn to his despite her determination not to look at him.

'That first-day feeling.' The wry smile that had nearly undone her before reappeared, curving his mouth and tightening the knot deep inside her. 'Will the patients like me? Will I fit in? Please God I don't make any mistakes.'

A lump formed in Polly's throat. She hadn't anticipated him being so honest—that he had admitted his worry and doubt made her like him even more. Instead of hiding behind some macho façade, he had exposed an inner part of himself, revealing unexpected vulnerability.

'I've been here nine weeks and I still have moments when I feel like that,' she told him, her voice huskier than normal as she matched his honesty with her own.

Dusky lashes lifted and the expression in his eyes, the unique sense of oneness, took her breath away. The intense connection seemed to last an eternity, and was broken only when Luca spoke.

'Nick said you were born in Penhally. Is there not a familiarity for you here?'

'Not really.' Polly bit her lip, unsure how much to tell him. What could she say? That she'd always felt on the outside, looking in? That she'd never belonged? She shook her head, more at herself than at him. 'I left a long time ago, so I doubt people would remember me.'

The slow smile that curved his mouth was brief but incredibly sexy. 'I cannot believe that anyone, having met you, would forget you, Polly.'

Luca's words had a disturbing effect, unexpectedly cracking open the vault in her head into which she'd consigned things she wanted to banish from her memory. Luca didn't know it, but he couldn't be more wrong in his assessment. She'd never made much of a blip on anyone's radar, let alone left any kind of permanent impression.

Whoever had invented the saying 'Sticks and stones may break my bones but words can never hurt me' had got it all wrong. At least for her. There had been no sticks or stones but thirteen years of constant verbal abuse had shattered her already shaky self-esteem. *Plain Polly from Penhally.* The once-familiar taunt returned to her with a suddenness that stole her breath. Worse, tears stung her eyes. Tears she refused to shed at thirty, just as she'd fought against them from the age of four…determined, even then, not to show any outward signs of weakness. She'd lived with the incessant stabbing pain before. She could do so again.

'Polly? What's wrong?'

Concern laced Luca's voice, but Polly shook her head in denial and resolutely avoided looking at him. She was shocked that after meeting only minutes ago, he should be so adept at reading her, so attuned to her inner feelings when she was quite sure nothing showed on the outside. Hiding her emotions was a technique she had perfected from a very young age.

She was saved from replying, or from Luca probing further,

because a knock at the door announced the arrival of their first patient. Polly called for them to come in and rose to her feet, finding her knees still too shaky to hold her. What she needed was to refocus her mind and, if not entirely forget that Luca was there, at least be distracted enough by the patient now opening the door not to notice the effect Luca had on her.

'Hello, Mr Murray. Do come in and take a seat.'

Polly fixed a public smile on her face as she offered her greeting. In the nine weeks she had been working here, very few people had recognised her or commented on her return. Which suited her just fine. But how ironic, after Luca's comments just moments ago, that the first patient of their joint surgery together should the father of a girl who had been in her class at school. Not that she expected Mr Murray to remember her—she and Dawn had never had much to do with each other. True, Dawn had teased her a time or two, but she had been nowhere near the worst. And how she had envied Dawn her closeness with her father.

As the sixty-year-old man with greying hair and a distinct stoop to his shoulders shuffled rather than walked into the room, Polly stepped around the desk and went to his aid. She remembered him as a robust, active and jolly man, so it was a huge shock to see how much he had aged in the years since she had last seen him.

'Thank you, Dr Polly.' Mr Murray's smile was warm but tired as he took the arm she offered.

Guiding him to a chair, Polly noted the dark circles under his pale green eyes, as well as the shallowness and raspy sound of his breathing. Clearly there had been no improvement since his last consultation. And now it was up to her to root out what lay behind the man's recurring chest infections. After ensuring he was comfortable, she introduced him to Luca—a quiet presence in the room but one she was continually aware of.

'Mr Murray, this is Dr Luca d'Azzaro.' It took a supreme effort of will, but Polly managed not to look at her new colleague, fearful of becoming trapped by the inexplicable pull he held on her. 'He's joined the medical team today, and is sitting in on a few consultations to familiarise himself with the practice system. Is that all right?'

'Fine by me,' Mr Murray agreed with a smile and a nod towards Luca.

'Dr Donnelly—Adam—suggested I take over from him in providing your care,' Polly continued, again ensuring that none of her inner feelings showed in her expression, 'but if you would rather see someone else, I—'

Mr Murray was swift to interrupt her. 'Goodness, no! Dr Adam gave me the choice, and when I heard you were back in Penhally as a GP, I asked to see you.'

'You did?'

The information took Polly completely by surprise and a lump formed in her throat as she absorbed his words, unable to doubt the sincerity of them. So thrown was she by the knowledge that anyone had specifically asked for her that her mask momentarily slipped before she could regather her composure.

She cleared her throat and tried to find her voice. 'Thank you, Mr Murray.'

'Please, call me Sandy,' he requested, encompassing them both, before a coughing fit overtook him, stripping the smile from his face and replacing it with evident discomfort.

This time Polly couldn't help but glance at Luca, noting that the same concern she felt was reflected in his dark eyes. As she passed Sandy a couple of tissues from the box she kept on her desk, Luca rose to his feet and crossed the room to pour a glass of cool water. When he returned, he rested his hand on the man's shoulder, a gesture of silent support and comfort, waiting until the coughing had subsided and he had gathered himself together before passing over the glass.

Polly's insides warmed at Luca's instinctive caring. It would be so much easier to harden her heart and ignore the fizzing attraction if he wasn't so damn likeable!

'Thanks.' Sandy's voice was rough after the bout of coughing. 'Sorry about that.'

'There is nothing to apologise for,' Polly reassured him, sending Luca a grateful smile as he returned to his chair, her heart jolting as he smiled back.

She had studied Sandy's notes after Adam had spoken to her the day before he had left, and now she handed them to Luca, hoping he would see what she did. As Luca looked through the medical history, Polly gathered her thoughts and focused on the patient.

'Sandy, have things been much the same since your last appointment with Dr Donnelly?' she asked now, eager to hear the patient's point of view.

'Worse, if anything. This is as bad as it's ever been. I feel I've aged about twenty years in the last two,' Sandy confided, his raw chuckle at odds with the tiredness and flicker of fear in his eyes.

Luca caught her gaze and signalled that he would like to ask a question. Appreciating his consideration and grateful for his input, Polly nodded.

'How did all this start, Sandy? Have you always had chest problems, or is it something that has come on gradually?' Luca queried. 'A quick glance at the notes now tells me you used to be a smoker.'

'Aye, I'm afraid so. Forty a day since the age of fifteen. Back then we didn't know it was bad for you,' he admitted with a sigh.

Polly listened as Sandy told them about his job, which had

involved him welding in confined spaces—a known trigger for chest problems—and how he had taken early retirement when it had become apparent that the work was having a detrimental affect on his health.

'My chest has worsened over the last two years. The cough has become more persistent and I can't ever shake it off. In the last few months I've had recurring bouts of bronchitis. Dr Adam convinced me that smoking was contributing to my health problems and persuaded me to stop. I haven't had a cigarette since.'

'Which is a fantastic achievement,' Luca praised him.

Polly added her agreement. 'Well done, Sandy. It's not easy breaking a lifelong habit.'

'Aye, well, I can't say that I've noticed much benefit from it.' His smile was wry, his voice maintaining a trace of his Scottish ancestry. 'I've gone from being an active man who enjoyed life to one who gets breathless after walking even a short distance. And then I get these chest infections on top of the wretched cough.'

Polly could see how much it was taking out of him, physically and emotionally. 'It must be very wearing. I'm not surprised you're fed up with it.'

Unable to resist, Polly's gaze was drawn to Luca. A tingle feathered down her spine as she looked into sinful dark eyes, and it was a struggle to drag hers free from his magnetic hold. She sucked in a shaky breath. Then promptly lost every scrap of air her lungs had managed to inhale as Luca touched her. One fingertip rested on the inside of her wrist. That was all. Yet her skin was on fire. Her pulse throbbed in her veins and a current of electricity sparked to every nerve ending. Luca apparently felt it, too, as he snatched his hand back as if scalded. Again her gaze clashed with his, the flare of awareness frightening in its suddenness and intensity.

Luca cleared his throat and looked down. Polly followed suit and saw the notepad he turned towards her. She bit her lip, trying to force away the strange and unwanted responses to the man as she concentrated on her job. She was unsurprised to discover that the four letters he had written with a question mark after it them mirrored her own thoughts in terms of Sandy's diagnosis. Nodding, she turned back to her patient, focusing on him and trying to ignore the way the pad of Luca's finger seemed to have permanently branded her.

Polly picked up her stethoscope and, after taking Sandy's blood pressure and his pulse, she listened to his chest, unsurprised by her findings. Next she discovered some swelling in his ankles, which he told her had been happening over the last couple of months. A gentle press with her fingers produced pitting in the skin that confirmed the oedema.

'Did Dr Donnelly talk to you about what might be wrong, Sandy?' she asked, not wanting to scare the man but needing him to be informed and actively involved in making decisions about his care.

Frowning, Sandy took another sip of his water. 'The last time he said that if things hadn't improved he would send me for a chest X-ray.'

'That's right. It would be wise you for to have that X-ray, Sandy. And I'd like to book you in for a few other tests as well.'

'Like what?' he queried, anxiety making his breathing sound faster and rougher.

Polly perched on the edge of the desk close to him. 'I'd like to do a blood test, and I want you to have a lung-function test. It's called spirometry—it's a bit like a breath test—and it accurately measures the air-flow obstruction and gauges the severity of the problem.'

'And what *is* the problem?' Sandy asked, his tension obvious.

Polly reached out and laid a hand on his arm. 'Chronic obstructive pulmonary disease, or COPD, is the rather grand umbrella title used to cover diseases like chronic bronchitis and emphysema. The symptoms can be like asthma, but it's a completely different condition. It's common, especially among those who are, or have been, smokers, exacerbated by certain jobs like yours. Put in simple terms, it causes a narrowing of the airways, preventing you from breathing properly. COPD is classified in stages, and we need to assess which group you fall into so that we can plan a proper course of treatment to help you.'

Sandy released a raspy breath. 'And can this COPD thing be cured?'

'No, I'm afraid not,' she told him honestly, giving his arm a gentle squeeze. 'Any damage already done can't be repaired, but what we *can* do is try to prevent things getting worse and help keep the symptoms in check.' Polly paused a moment, her gaze sliding of its own accord to Luca, her heart skipping as he smiled, approval and support foremost in his eyes. Feeling breathless herself, Polly continued. 'There are various things we can do in terms of medication, inhalers and short- or long-acting drugs. You've already taken a big step by stopping smoking and preventing further damage. Once we know what we're dealing with, we can talk again and decide what is best for you.'

'It's a lot to take in,' Sandy murmured with a shake of his head.

Polly smiled in sympathy. 'I know. But you can come and see me, or phone me, at any time if you have questions, and we'll be here to work through this with you, Sandy,' she promised him.

'My wife will be worried when I tell her,' he said, a frown creasing his brow.

'By all means bring her with you next time and I'll be happy to explain to her.' Polly straightened and went to her filing cabinet, removing a couple of leaflets from a folder. 'These will give you both the basic information. Once we've put a treatment plan in place, I'd like you to have the annual flu vaccination and also an immunisation against pneumo-coccus, which is a germ that causes a chest infection. We want to guard against you picking up anything else,' she explained. 'It's also important for you to do some regular exercise once we have things under control—a brisk walk each day would be good. Anything that helps to improve your breathing. Lauren, our physiotherapist, will help you with that.'

Polly returned to her chair and jotted down a few notes. 'Are you able to get to the hospital in St Piran for the X-ray?' she asked.

'Aye, that won't be a problem,' Sandy confirmed. 'My wife or son will take me. I'm not looking forward to telling my daughter what's going on. You remember Dawn, don't you, Dr Polly, love? She was in your class at school.'

'Yes, of course. How is she?' Polly asked, her guard in place, her smile polite.

'Grand, she is! Married now and living in Canada. She'll be pleased to have news of you.'

Conscious of Luca listening in, Polly hurried to bring the subject back to Sandy and his health. 'We'll make an ap-pointment for you to see one of the practice nurses for the blood test and the spirometry, and when we have the results of those, and the X-ray, I'll see you again and we can discuss the options. In the meantime I'm adjusting your prescription to help relieve some of your symptoms.'

'Thanks so much, you're a grand girl,' Sandy told her with a smile.

Embarrassed, Polly rose to her feet to escort him out. 'I'll see you in a week or so, Sandy. But don't forget I'm here if there is anything troubling you.'

'I won't forget. You've both been very kind and helpful.' At the door, he paused and shook her hand, then nodded to Luca. 'Welcome to Penhally, Doctor.'

'Thank you, Sandy. I am already finding my time here very interesting and enlightening.'

Luca's response made Polly tense. His huskily accented voice affected her, but his words made her wary as she very much feared he was referring to more than his interest in Sandy's condition. Having stopped by the reception desk to ensure that Sandy made an appointment to see practice nurse Gemma as soon as possible, Polly asked Sue to send the next patient through. Then she had no excuse not to return to her consulting room. Her nerves were jangling as she prepared herself for seeing Luca again.

He was standing with his back to her, looking out of the window, his hands thrust into the pockets of his trousers. Polly paused, drinking in the imposing sight of him, so masculine, so attractive, so disturbing. She didn't know what was happening between them, but as Luca turned and his gaze met hers, a surge of electricity shot through her. If the expression in his dark eyes was anything to go by, he was as confused and wary and unwelcoming of the attraction as she was.

She knew nothing about him, had met him only a short time ago, and yet she very much feared Luca d'Azzaro was going to turn her already turbulent life upside down.

CHAPTER THREE

'I'M FULLY aware of the pressure on beds but that doesn't excuse discharging a patient so soon after an open cholecystomy, especially when they live alone and have no back-up assistance whatsoever. It isn't going to help the hospital's bed situation if the patient is brought back to St Piran's A and E department in an ambulance with complications requiring readmission, is it?'

Luca smothered a grin as he listened to Polly politely but firmly express her point of view. With the patient's cordless telephone in one hand and the other sketching occasional gestures in the air, she paced the bedroom in the small bungalow, looking for all the world like a brave and bold Valkyrie throwing herself into battle—well, she would if she had a few more inches in height and considerably more weight on her tiny frame.

Glancing at their patient, a fifty-five-year-old widow who had undergone an emergency operation to remove her gall bladder, Luca agreed with the stand Polly was taking. Sitting on the side of Delia Hocking's bed, he held her clammy, trembling hand, sharing Polly's anger that some error or misjudgement had caused Delia to be sent home without adequate analgesia and before she had even eaten anything. Now, aside from the pain, Delia was nauseous—not uncommon after such an operation—and there was some bleeding from the wound. Thankfully, there was no sign of infection. Yet. The risk was there, however, so he and Polly had erred on the side of caution and prescribed some prophylactic antibiotics.

'Maybe you consider that nibbling on half a digestive biscuit is eating proper food, but I'm afraid I don't,' Polly said now, resuming her pacing, a frown on her face as she listened to the person on the other end of the line.

Delia met his gaze. Although her face was grey with pain and exhaustion, humour brought a twinkle of amusement to her hazel eyes. 'Feisty little thing, isn't she?'

'That she is,' Luca agreed with a smile.

Admiration welling within him, his focus strayed back to Polly who was standing by the window, the toes of one sandalled foot tapping the carpeted floor with impatience. Despite his determination to ignore the intense reaction he had felt for her from the moment they had met, his interest and fascination had grown with each day that passed. Now it was Thursday, his fourth day working at the surgery, and while he had come to know Polly extremely well as a doctor, he had discovered frustratingly little about her personally, apart from basic tastes in books, music and that sort of thing.

What meagre details he had gleaned had been thanks mostly to colleagues, especially in the staffroom, where questions had been asked and confidences shared. Everyone had been friendly and welcoming, helping him find his place at the surgery, and it was thanks to the general chat and the occasional moment of indiscretion that he knew that this was the first time Polly had returned to Penhally since leaving at the age of seventeen. He had also learned that Carrick was her mother's maiden name, but no one seemed certain about why or when she had undertaken the change of surname, although rumour suggested that she had, at one time, been married. Whether that meant she was widowed, divorced or separated, he had not yet ascertained.

Luca wanted to know more, much more, but he had declined to ask...so for. Although his list of questions was rapidly multiplying. Polly chose to melt into the background, hoping not to be noticed. Why? At first he'd wondered if it was just him she was wary of, but he'd soon discovered she was the same with everyone. Polly was fiercely private—a trait they shared—and, as she had refrained from probing into his life, so he had shown her the same respect. He was hoping that, in time, she would come to trust him and would freely volunteer some of her secrets.

That Polly was an incredible doctor had been apparent from that first consultation with Sandy Murray. She was a wonderful listener, empathetic and instinctive, and adept at assessing what patients responded to—an arm around the shoulder, a challenge to motivate them, or a push to face up to reality and to take back control of their lives and their bodies. She wanted the best for them and she gave of herself to help them. And Delia was right about the feistiness. Polly gave total support to her patients, fighting battles for them and prepared to take on their problems.

Nick had told him Polly was good with young teenagers, but as far as he could see she was wonderful with everyone, young and old alike. The only times he had seen her in any way uncomfortable and forced was with young children. He didn't believe for a moment that she disliked them, but she was certainly awkward with the younger ones around the age of his twins. He had yet to work out why. In his experience, children were excellent judges of character, and they gravitated to Polly, just as everyone else did, but there was a definite reserve from her. It was yet one more puzzle to figure out about her.

Rosie and Toni were his top priority. Everything he did was for them. And *if* there was ever to be anyone in his life in future, they would have to love the girls, and the girls them. But that was no more in his plans than flying to the moon, and he had not so much as noticed another woman since Elaine had died...until Polly.

Luca's insides squeezed with pain and guilt and confusion, just as they always did when he thought of Elaine. Then came the lance of hurt at what she had done. He didn't want anyone new in his life, he hadn't even thought about it. So why now? And why, of all women, was it Polly who had captured his attention? In build and colouring she was definitely not the type of woman he had been attracted to before Elaine. And she was nothing like adventurous, outgoing Elaine, who had been tall and athletic, with womanly curves, dark auburn hair and green eyes. But his body appeared to have a will of its own. It was rousing itself from a long—and, he had thought, permanent—hibernation, and, inexplicably, Polly was the was the woman making it happen.

He didn't *want* this. But day by day he was in deeper and deeper trouble, more and more intrigued by Polly. He couldn't explain it. He didn't understand it. But somehow, from the first moment of meeting her, his inner radar had been plugged directly into Polly's frequency. Not just in physical terms with the searing sexual attraction between them, although his body's instinctive response to her was irrefutable, but... He couldn't find the right word. Not emotionally, or even mentally. More spiritually, which sounded completely wacky and off the wall. But how else to explain the fact that although Polly presented a smiling face and an air of outward calm to the world—and anyone looking at her would think she was fine—he knew it was an act, a public face, hiding her emotions, presenting a serene façade quite at odds to how she was feeling within.

How did he know that? How could he see what no one else could? Things Polly didn't want them to see. He didn't know how, but he sensed when she was unsettled or upset, as had happened with Sandy Murray on Monday when the man had mentioned Polly's past.

His heart skipped a beat as he looked at her now, standing illuminated in a patch of sunlight by the window, her wavy ash-blonde hair falling loose around her shoulders. Her style of dress was unique. She put colours together that ought to clash horribly, but on her they looked right. Long gypsy skirts—today's was a patchwork of purples—several layers of assorted tops that threatened to swamp her, and, on her feet, sandals with little or no heel.

Luca's gaze journeyed down, paused at the flash of bare ankles that looked far too slender to hold her upright, and then he noticed the delicate feet and the purple-painted toenails. His gut tightened. *Dio!* Now he was developing a toe fetish. The attempt to mock himself failed, and it was a struggle to force his gaze upwards again, where it paused at the collection of assorted bangles on her right wrist that jangled softly as she moved, before returning to her expressive face as she talked.

One word had popped unbidden into his head when he had first met Polly on Monday and, despite trying to keep his distance from her, mentally and physically, he found himself thinking of her by the nickname all the time. *Zingarella*…little gypsy in Italian.

Time was flying by. He'd been taking his own consultations since Tuesday and had told himself he was relieved to be spending less time in Polly's company, but no matter how many times he told himself he wasn't interested, he found himself looking for her, listening for the sound of her voice and waiting impatiently for the hours they spent together doing home visits, which then rushed by far too quickly. Already the first week was nearly over. One more and he would be on his own and opportunities to work with Polly would be restricted.

Thankfully, after Monday their journeys out together had been undertaken in his car, but today it had let him down, developing a mechanical fault that meant it was now in the local garage, being fixed. It also meant he'd had to break a promise to himself never to get in Polly's car again. It was nothing to do with her driving. It was simply far too cramped, increasing his awareness and confining them so closely that he inhaled the subtle but intoxicating scent of her with every breath—a flowery, old-fashioned scent he couldn't immediately name. But it was heady and sexy and drove him crazy. At least his four-wheel-drive—roomy enough to accommodate two growing girls and their assorted stuff—afforded sufficient space that Polly wasn't brushing against him with every gear change or turn of the steering wheel.

'Yes, of course I'm still waiting!'

Polly's words pulled him from his thoughts and refocused his attention. The exasperation as she responded to the person on the other end of the line was obvious. She turned around and paced back towards the bed. Meeting his gaze, she rolled her eyes, sharing several moments of deep connection before returning her attention to their patient and leaving him trying to regain his equilibrium.

'Don't worry, Delia,' she said, covering the mouthpiece of the phone with one hand and sending the woman a warm smile. 'I'm not sending you back to St Piran's unless absolutely unavoidable. I just need to shake them up a bit.'

Luca couldn't help but smile at the image of this half-pint-sized young woman taking on the stubborn bureaucracy of the hospital administrators.

Hearing Delia's moan of pain as she tried to reach out with her free hand for a glass of water, Luca moved to make her more comfortable, supporting her as he held the glass for her. 'Just take a few sips,' he advised her, concerned that too much water too soon might aggravate her nausea.

'I'm sorry to put everyone to this bother,' Delia apologised, the catch in her voice betraying how raw and close to the surface her emotions lay.

'You're *not* a bother, Delia,' Polly insisted. 'None of this is your fault. We want the best for you.' She hesitated a moment, then smothered a curse. 'If they put me on hold again, I'm going to scream!'

Leaving Polly to focus on her call, Luca took over the task of reassuring Delia. He explained the arrangements he and Polly had already put in place, including switching Delia to stronger painkillers and prescribing an anti-sickness medication as well as the antibiotics.

'Someone will come in morning and night to assist you, and Rebecca Grey, one of Penhally's district nurses, will call in every day to begin with to check your dressing,' he told her, smiling at her surprised expression. 'Polly has spoken with the two neighbours you're friendly with, and both are eager to help with anything you need, so don't be afraid to ask. And ring the surgery any time. OK?'

Tears moistened Delia's lashes. 'Thank you. You've both been terrific.'

Polly finished her call with the hospital and sat down to speak with Delia. When Polly's mobile phone rang, Luca offered to answer it, and was rewarded with the kind of smile that set his blood on fire and made him think things he had not thought about for a very long time. Disturbed by her affect on him, he picked up the phone and stepped out of the room.

'Oh, hi, Luca,' Chloe greeted him as he answered the call. 'I'm sorry to bother you. We have a bit of a crisis.'

* * *

Kate Althorp walked slowly through St Piran Hospital, a place she had become far too familiar with since July and which, after tomorrow, she hoped never to spend time in again. Not as a patient, anyway.

Tomorrow was the last day of her radiotherapy, a necessary treatment after a successful lumpectomy had removed a cancerous growth from her breast but one she had endured the last five weeks and which had left her tired, emotional and with other side-effects like a dry mouth, sore throat and a rash. And, as she approached the end of her treatment, there had been some redness and blistering of the skin. Still, as Rob had said, at least she hadn't been horribly sick.

Thinking about Rob made her smile. And yet she also felt a touch of sadness. He had been so wonderful to her and she had come to care deeply for him, appreciating the fact that, for the first time in years, she didn't have to carry every burden alone. But always at the back of her mind, lurking and tormenting, was the spectre of Nick and his inability to face up to the reality of Jem and his responsibilities.

She hadn't seen Nick since he had come to the hospital after her operation, and she knew he was avoiding her. Just as she knew, thanks to comments from various visitors, that Nick was ever more aloof at work, his moods uncertain, largely due to burning the candle at both ends and apparently working his way through many of the available women in Cornwall. It was none of her business—but it hurt.

Approaching the front doors, where she had arranged to meet Chloe, Kate tried to set Nick aside. It did no good to dwell on him. He found it impossible to give her what she needed, whereas Rob was the exact opposite. He treated Jem the same way he did Matthew, his own son. And, for her, Jem's well-being took priority over everything else.

'Hi, Kate.'

'Polly!'

It took a moment for Kate to adjust her thoughts. Polly was not just her goddaughter but like a younger sister and, most definitely, a friend. Seeing her here now brought a flash of concern at the unexpected change of plan.

'Is everything all right? What's happened to Chloe?'

Polly smiled, linking arms as they walked side by side towards the main doors. 'Chloe's fine. She's sorry not to come herself but even though she isn't on duty, she was called to one of her mums and an emergency delivery.'

'Oh, dear. I do hope mother and baby will be all right.' Worry was uppermost as they stepped outside into the warm September air.

'Chloe says everything is fine,' Polly reassured. 'Luca and I were halfway between here and Penhally on our final home visit, so it was no trouble to come and collect you. And Oliver is taking over for tomorrow because I haven't been able to escape this wretched talk Nick's arranged for me at the school.'

'You'll do fine, my love,' Kate reassured her, hiding her own concern about Polly going back there.

Polly shivered. 'I hope so. About Nick...' she added after a pause.

'What about him?' Kate asked, wariness setting her nerves on edge.

'Chloe said the only other person able to collect you was Nick, and you would rather he didn't.' Kate noted Polly's in-decision as she paused and bit her lip. 'Not that I'm sorry to come myself, but I was puzzled. You and Nick were always good friends. Has something happened?'

'It's a long story—and one I'll explain once this week is over and we have some time alone,' Kate promised, dread settling like a lead weight in her stomach.

She owed the truth to Polly, of all people. Indeed, she had planned to confess when Polly had returned to Penhally but the events of the last weeks had pushed all other things from her mind. She couldn't put off the unsavoury task much longer. Despite the September sunshine, Kate shivered. Polly had been fond of James, and Kate didn't relish the prospect of telling her how she, Kate, had betrayed him on the night he'd died. Fresh tears, which seemed to flow all too readily these last few weeks, beaded her lashes.

'Oh, Kate, I didn't mean to upset you!' the younger woman exclaimed.

'You haven't. It's not you, Polly. I seem to cry over nothing at the moment,' Kate joked with a forced smile, eager to change the subject.

As they approached the car, the passenger door opened and a stunningly handsome man emerged. Kate saw the expression in the man's dark eyes as he looked at Polly, and felt Polly stiffen in response. Glancing from one to the other, Kate felt a dart of hope shoot through her. Oh! If only… Polly had been through so much, both as a child and an adult, and from what Kate had heard about the new doctor he, too, had suffered heartache. From the looks of things, they were both fighting the attraction between them, but Kate wished with all her heart that Polly, who so deserved it, would find a way to open herself up to happiness.

'Now, my love,' she said, noting the tinge of colour warming Polly's pale cheeks, 'I presume this is Luca, our new GP?'

Polly drove out the hospital car park and headed in the direction of Penhally, relieved that Kate and Luca were making small talk, absolving her of the need to join in. She had been thrown by the change of plans, and Chloe's call for help had left Polly anxious. Although Kate was usually the soul of discretion, Polly felt uneasy bringing Luca along, with the risk of opening up other aspects of her life to him.

She'd been relieved to get Monday over and for Luca to be taking his own consultations, although she still had over a week of joint home visits to survive. In the last few days she'd discovered that Luca was a fabulous doctor, medically skilled and wonderful with patients, setting young and old at ease. Polly took a surreptitious peep at him in the rear-view mirror. If only he was horrible she would be able to forget him and ignore the good looks. But he wasn't. He was funny, kind and smart. He had the uncanny ability to read her with ease, to see beyond the smile... And he fired her blood in a way no other man had ever done. She forced herself to ignore it because she didn't understand it and she didn't want an involvement with anyone, especially someone with children the age of Luca's.

After being introduced to Kate, he'd been a total gentleman, charming her and giving up the front seat so she would be more comfortable—even though that meant his athletically muscled body was cramped in the rear of the car. He'd then faced the issue of Kate's situation with a directness and a gentleness that Kate had clearly appreciated. And anything that made Kate happy and set her at ease met with Polly's approval.

The older woman had always been strong, coming through whatever life had thrown at her, but Polly knew this was the toughest thing Kate had faced—along with the death of her husband James. Polly was very proud of her friend. She was also relieved that, however difficult things might be for her, facing up to the past and searching for a place where she fitted in, fate had brought her back to Penhally at the very moment Kate had needed all her friends around her.

'Yes,' Kate was saying, in answer to a question from Luca, drawing Polly's attention back to the conversation. 'Tomorrow is my final day of rads, and it can't come soon enough.'

'The last three months must have been an ordeal for you, not to mention very scary,' Polly heard Luca sympathise, the sound of his voice sending a wave of tingles skittering down her spine.

'It's not been easy,' Kate admitted. As Polly halted at a road junction, Kate briefly laid a hand on her arm and smiled. 'But everyone has been wonderfully kind and supportive, especially my little Polly.'

Feeling emotional, and very aware of Luca's presence behind her, Polly shook her head. 'I haven't done anything much.'

'Oh, but you *have*, my love. Aside from organising the rota for these last two weeks of visits to St Piran's, setting my mind, and Rob's, to rest, just having you here at last, and being able to see you every day, has been so wonderful for me.'

'Kate…'

'The timing couldn't have been worse, of course,' her friend continued, her lack of discretion in front of Luca making Polly intensely uncomfortable. 'I've been so worried about you, and feel as if I've abandoned you. I persuaded you to come back here, after all, and then the minute you do, I'm not around for you…more like the wicked witch than your kind godmother!'

Any hope that Luca might not have heard was dashed when Polly had a quick peep in the rear-view mirror and met his enigmatic dark gaze. She had the eerie feeling that he could see inside her right to her soul. Frightened, she dragged her gaze away and tried to compose herself.

'You didn't ask for this to happen, Kate,' Polly murmured after a moment, focusing on the road and reminding herself not to look at Luca again. 'And there was nowhere else I would have wanted to be but here with you when you were going through this.'

'Bless you, my love.' Kate's voice sounded heavy with emotion. 'You can deny it all you like, but you've done so much for me these last weeks.'

'A mere blip compared with all you have done for me all my life, not just as my godmother but my friend,' Polly replied, hugely relieved when Kate changed direction.

'Jem was my main worry. How can a ten-year-old get to grips with something like this? But he's been tremendous.' Kate half turned in her seat to bring Luca into the conversation. 'Having raised my son alone, I have every admiration for you, Luca. I understand you have twin girls? I imagine that's double the trouble.'

'They can be a handful. And they gang up on me to get their own way!' he confided with a chuckle.

Polly heard the amusement and the love in Luca's voice and a new, even larger lump formed in her throat. Staffroom gossip had furnished the information that Luca's wife had died having the twins. She had tried not to think about the pain he had gone through, tried, too, not to think about two girls without their mother, of the parallels—and differences—with her childhood, and of now and what never could be. Countless times she had told herself not to think of Luca at all, or of his girls, forcing herself to ignore and resist the undeniable attraction she felt but which she knew could never come to anything. But nothing worked. She could not put him out of her mind.

'How old are your girls, Luca?' Kate was asking now, and Polly braced herself against the smart of hurt that she knew would come, along with the despair and the longing and the insidious nagging guilt.

'Rosie and Toni are three—and they'd insist I add the all-important "three-quarters".' Another throaty, sexy chuckle rumbled from his chest, and despite the riot of emotions roiling within her, the sound teased her, inflaming every nerve ending. 'They'll be four in January.'

'Ah. I see.'

Polly heard the tone of Kate's voice and knew she was

looking at her, but she stared studiously ahead, refusing to react, scared in case she made a fool of herself in front of Luca. A silence fell, one that now felt charged, and Polly was uncomfortably aware of Luca behind her, concerned in case anything Kate had divulged would register with him. Her pulse was rapid, she could feel it throb at the base of her neck, and her chest felt tighter and tighter as she tried to contain the confusing mixture of feelings that threatened to press in on her. Old memories and old pain, stirred up by her return to Penhally, clashed with more recent heartbreak and turmoil. And now, thrown into the cauldron to be jumbled up with the rest, was everything relating to Luca...

The unwanted attraction.

The assault on her senses.

And his daughters.

She needed desperately to be alone right now to sort things through in her head and get her emotions and her memories under control. Hopefully the remainder of the journey back to Penhally would be completed quickly and without further incident. But they had barely covered another mile when Kate spoke again.

'Lilacs!'

Taken completely by surprise, Polly frowned. 'I'm sorry?'

'Your scent. I knew I recognised it, but it's been such a long time since I smelled it,' Kate told her. 'It's just hit me. Lilacs— it's what your mother used to wear.'

'Yes.'

The whispered word escaped her lips. So many things about her mother had faded from her memory and she hated it that she could not draw on more, that she had nothing more of her to touch and to remember, that she could not even recall her face. But she had only been four when her mother had died. She did remember the lilacs, and all her life their scent had reminded her of the mother she had loved so much and lost so young. It was something she could wrap herself in, like an invisible comfort blanket. She had worn it since she had struck out on her own when she had been seventeen, trying to keep what she could of her mother close to her.

Kate reached out again and lightly brushed her arm. 'Yvonne would have been so proud of you, my love. Just as I am. As if you were my own daughter.'

Polly was unable to force any response past the restriction in her throat, and her fingers tightened around the steering-wheel as she fought back the sudden tears that threatened to blur her vision.

'When I feel up to it, Rob's going to help me go through the stuff I've been hoarding in the attic,' Kate continued, resting her head back against the seat, her tiredness evident. 'There are some things there that I packed away a long time ago—now you might like to have them.'

Polly sucked in a ragged breath, trying to steady herself and not be too hopeful in case of further disappointment. 'Kate, do you have any photos of my mother?'

'I know there are some amongst the attic treasures. If there are any you haven't already got, I can get you some copies done,' Kate offered.

'I don't have any.'

Sitting cramped in the back of the too-small car, Luca had to strain to hear Polly's words she was talking so quietly. Kate turned to look at her and, in profile, he saw her frown of confusion. 'Your mum had albums full of photos. She loved them. You used to sit on her lap and beg her to tell you the stories behind each one. Don't you remember?'

Polly nodded, but Luca saw her knuckles whiten as she clung to the steering-wheel. From where he was sitting, he could see the reflection of part of her face, but he was well aware of her tension, could hear it in her voice. It had been there when Kate had asked him about the twins, increasing when he had spoken of their ages, puzzling him, but it had now intensified and he felt the emotion coming off Polly in waves. She hid it well, but it unsettled him that he knew how she was feeling, unsettled him, too, that despite knowing he should leave well alone and keep away from Polly, he wanted to hold her, to comfort her, to unravel her mysteries and find out what was wrong. He had no idea what was upsetting her but it felt, to him, as if she was at the end of her tether.

'I'd love to see those albums again,' Kate continued, apparently oblivious of Polly's inner distress, although it was shouting out at him. 'Do you have them?'

'No.'

'Oh, that's a shame. Whatever could have happened to them?' Kate mused.

Luca wanted to tell Kate to stop. Could she not see that her questions were upsetting Polly?

He leaned forward, catching the sweetness of Polly's scent, able to identify it now, learning the significance of it for Polly. Her hands were still tightly clenched and her face was pale. She headed the car down the hill and into the centre of Penhally to the sea, before turning left out of Bridge Street and into Harbour Road, driving around half of the horseshoe-shaped seafront. As they neared the surgery, Polly turned left again and, within moments they had covered the short distance up to Kate's house and were drawing into the kerb outside.

'Polly? What is it?'

The anxiety in Kate's voice alerted him, and Luca shifted closer.

For a moment Polly sat still, staring straight ahead. Then she spoke. 'The albums. He burned them.'

Although the words were whispered, they seemed to echo loudly in the confines of the car.

'Oh, Polly.' Kate sucked in a breath, pressing one hand to her throat, her other hand once more going out to rest on Polly's arm. 'I'm sorry, my love. I never thought.'

Polly shook her head and scrambled out of the car. As Kate rummaged in her handbag, Luca opened the rear door and, feeling a bit like a sardine escaping a tin can, he eased himself out and stretched his limbs. He and Polly reached for the passenger door's handle at the same moment. The brief brush of flesh on flesh before Polly snatched her hand away was enough to leave him feeling singed, sending a charge of electricity and desire shooting through him. *Dio!* He had to get a grip.

As Polly stood back, clearly not wanting a repetition, any more than he did, he opened the door for Kate and held out his hand to help her out. 'Thank you, Luca.' The older woman smiled up at him, but he could see how exhausted she was.

He was surprised when Kate lingered, maintaining her hold on his arm. In her free hand she had her keys, and she held them out to Polly.

'Would you mind getting the front door open for me?' she asked.

Polly looked puzzled but did as Kate asked. 'No problem,' she agreed, taking the keys.

When Polly had crossed the pavement and opened the gate, Kate turned to him. 'Luca, watch out for Polly.'

No matter how many times he told himself he wanted nothing to do with Polly beyond a friendly working relationship, with each moment spent in her company, he wanted to know more about her. The nagging feeling persisted that beneath her serene exterior something wasn't right—and now, hearing Kate's concern, he knew he would not be able to keep his distance.

The relationship between Polly and Kate was a very close and special one. From the conversation in the car, and the fact that Kate was Polly's godmother, it was obvious that Kate had been friends with Polly's mother and, of course, had known Polly as a child. What had happened back then? Why was Polly upset? And who had burned something Polly had treasured?

The more he found out about Polly, the less he knew and the more questions he had that needed answers. Why had Polly left the village all those years ago? All this time later, Kate had persuaded a reluctant Polly to come back to Penhally. Why now? And why had Polly needed persuading?

'Kate?' Polly called from the porch at the front of the pretty, whitewashed cottage.

'Just a minute, my love.'

Luca looked round at the exchange, his gaze resting on Polly. Even across the distance that separated them he could see the confusion and anxiety evident on her face. She looked small and fragile and exquisitely lovely. The heart he had been sure would never feel anything again clenched inside him. He should walk away. Before the twins got involved or anyone was hurt. Now, while he still could.

'Luca?'

Dragging his gaze from Polly, he looked down into Kate's eyes, seeing the worry and the plea in their depths, and he found himself nodding his head without making a conscious effort to do so.

'Thank you.'

Having secured his acceptance, Kate walked slowly up the path to join Polly. At the door, the two women hugged and as they drew back he saw Kate rest the palm of one hand against Polly's cheek. He couldn't hear what words were spoken, but everything about Polly's tiny frame screamed of aloneness and inner unhappiness. He had enough to contend with, com-

ing to terms with what Elaine had done and giving everything
to care for the girls as they began this new chapter of their lives
in Penhally. There was no room for anything or anyone else.

But as Polly walked back down the path towards him,
sapphire-blue eyes reflecting her confusion, unease and the
awareness she was fighting as hard as he was, he knew he was
already in too deep and that it was now too late to turn back.

CHAPTER FOUR

TO SAY she'd had reservations when Nick had sprung the young persons' drop-in clinic on her so soon after her arrival would have been an understatement, Polly admitted. Aside from being new to the medical team and not wanting to step on anyone's toes, there had been a nagging concern in the back of her mind that working closely with young teens here in Penhally might trigger memories she would sooner remain buried in the past where they belonged.

Having once committed to the project, however, Polly had thrown herself into it wholeheartedly. The surgery's community room was used for various groups and activities on different days of the week, including the new rape crisis centre, which Nick's niece, Charlotte, ran on a Wednesday. Furnished like a common room or large living room, with sofas and armchairs and occasional tables, it was an ideal venue for the teenagers, helping them feel relaxed and comfortable.

From the first day the clinic had opened in early August, it had been obvious that it had struck a chord with the local youth. More people came each week, and while some just looked around and took a few leaflets, others stayed, asked questions and joined in group discussions. A few took the opportunity for an informal but confidential chat in the private room next door about a wide range of things bothering them, from medical or emotional issues to family, friends or school problems.

Distracted, Polly stared out of the window, wondering what she would have done had a clinic like this been available when she had been a teenager. Her throat tightened, and she wrapped her arms around herself. There had been no similar resource back then. And with Reg preventing her from having regular access to Kate, the one person she might have been able to talk to, Polly had coped alone. With hindsight some of her choices had been poor ones, but she had survived. Sort of. She struggled to push back the past, refusing to let it take hold of her.

She dragged her focus back to today. It had been the busiest Saturday so far, and she had been grateful for an extra pair of hands…even though they had come in the disturbing form of Luca d'Azzaro. His presence had allowed her more one-on-one time with those who needed it. But when just so much as *thinking* of him made her blood heat and squeezed the aching knot deep inside her, having him around all the time kept her nerves jangling and her senses on red alert.

Frowning, Polly reflected on the situation with Luca. She was increasingly confused, especially as there had been a subtle change since Thursday's car journey with Kate. It was nothing she could put her finger on, but the charge between them felt more electric, and she was even more on edge and aware of him. She had met him less than a week ago and had tried hard to keep things on a purely professional footing, refusing to ask any personal questions or acknowledge her growing curiosity about him.

But no matter how much she reminded herself of the mis-judgements and mistakes she had made in the past, and of her promise to herself never to trust anyone again or give herself up for any other man, it was becoming more and more difficult to ignore her attraction and growing feelings for Luca. Which made her fearful that the shield she had worked so hard to create around herself was not as impenetrable as she had hoped. At least when it came to Luca.

Polly glanced up as the door of the community room opened and the object of her thoughts stepped into the room. Immediately she felt warmth bloom across her cheeks and hastily dragged her gaze from his, busying herself tidying up the stacks of leaflets to file them away and leave the room ready for the next group to use it.

'Hi,' Luca greeted her. 'That's the last of them away. I've just locked the main door.'

Polly nodded in acknowledgement, then looked down. She had left her hair loose today, hoping to appear more approachable for the youngsters, and now she welcomed the effect as it fell forward to screen her face. But her hands shook, betraying her, so she pulled them away, clasping them behind her out of sight.

'Thanks for your help, Luca. It's been a busy day.'

'I've enjoyed it. They're nice kids. And they're gaining so much from what you're doing for them,' he praised her.

'It was Nick's brainchild, not mine.' She frowned, still puzzled by the whole thing. 'I just wonder why he didn't set it up before.'

'Nick didn't have you before.'

The huskily accented voice, laced with both amusement and appreciation, made her chest feel tight. It was almost impossible to draw enough air into her lungs as Luca perched casually on the arm of a two-seater sofa nearby and smiled…a rare, slow, sexy smile that ought to come with a government health warning. Polly swallowed, trying not to notice the way faded jeans hugged the length of athletically muscled legs or how his grey jumper accentuated his colouring and masculinity.

Her blood pressure rose as she recalled how the hem of the

jumper had risen several times during the day as he had stretched, exposing a tantalising sliver of olive-toned skin— smooth at the back and sides but with an intriguing line of dark hair running down from his navel to disappear below the waistband of his jeans. Her fingers had itched to touch him and, feeling hot and bothered, she had to clench them together now to prevent them giving in to temptation.

Feeling jumpy, she longed to escape, but the only route to the door would necessitate her pushing past Luca. So she held her ground and tried to focus on the topic at hand and not on her runaway thoughts.

'I don't know that I have anything to do with it,' she protested.

'It has everything to do with you, *zingarella*.' Her heart throbbed under her ribs as he chuckled, and she bit her lip, wondering what he had called her. '*You* may not recognise it, but you have a special gift with people. And the youngsters gravitate to you and feel comfortable with you. That's what Nick saw—it's what I can see,' he added, dark eyes watching her intently. 'You have an instinctive knack of getting to the heart of what is troubling the teenagers, and you set them at ease. You have a natural empathy and ability to listen, you take on people's problems, and you inspire trust and confidence because you make them feel as if they matter.'

'Luca…'

Flustered, Polly broke off. She had no idea what to say. Aside from Kate, no one had ever believed in her before and that Luca, who had known her less than a week, could say these things with apparent sincerity confused her completely. It also made keeping him at a distance ever more difficult.

'I lost count of the number of people who said they had heard of the clinic but it was listening to your talk and meeting you at the school yesterday that convinced them to come. It's *you* they come for, Polly.'

The talk Nick had arranged with the headmaster and which Polly would have given anything to avoid. She had not expected Luca to accompany her, but he had. And, once more, he had been scarily sensitive to her emotions, picking up straight away on her nervousness and anxiety. He'd been supportive and understanding, although Polly felt a twinge of guilt that she hadn't corrected his assumption that her unease was because she didn't like to speak in public. Thankfully, he'd had no idea of the real reason for, or the extent of, her inner turmoil.

Aside from the surgery, she'd managed to stay away from any places in Penhally that might provoke memories she was not yet able to cope with. Until yesterday. Visiting the school had threatened to be worse than she had anticipated…had it not been for Luca.

Painful memories of her years growing up in Penhally had assailed her as soon as she had seen the building. For a few moments she had been frozen to the spot, scarcely able to breathe as the sudden weight of her past had crashed down on her. Luca had stopped beside her. He hadn't said a word, but had taken her hand in his and linked their fingers.

It was only now that she looked back on it with a clear head that she realised how she had clung to him, energised by the surge of electricity that had flowed between them, absorbing his strength, able to do what had to be done because he had been there beside her. And that frightened her. She had learned the lessons of the past and knew she could never again rely on anyone but herself, yet for those moments, with Luca, she had forgotten. For a short span of time she had not felt alone. And it had felt far too good.

Acutely aware that just thinking about his touch made her hand tingle all over again, she turned away from his steady, silent inspection, desperate to steer the conversation away from herself. Searching for something—anything—she remembered Nick's comments on the day Luca had arrived.

'I'm sure some of the teenagers, the boys in particular, felt more comfortable talking to a man and were glad you were here,' she murmured, fidgeting once more with the leaflets she still needed to put away. 'You have an interest, too.' Pausing, unable to help herself, she looked up and met his dark, watchful gaze. 'Why did you give up your ambition to be a paediatric surgeon?'

Luca felt the unexpected question like a body blow and it took a moment for him to catch his breath. Polly had neatly turned the tables on him, guarding her own secrets yet trying to expose his own. Had it been anyone else, he would have given the usual flippant answer to brush the enquirer off, but it was Polly who for the first time in the whole week had actually shown any sign of interest or asked him anything about himself. And because it was Polly, because he wanted her to trust him, to know him, despite the battle that still raged inside him against what he was beginning to feel for her, he told her the truth.

'Paediatric surgery, and working with the older children in particular, was my dream, and what I went into medicine to do,' he began, standing up and sinking his hands into the pockets of his jeans. 'I worked ludicrously long hours during my training to achieve my goal, extra hours that I could— *should*—have spent at home with Elaine. When she died…'

Luca paused, bracing himself, anticipating the customary stab of pain, confused and unsettled to find that it had dulled to a raw ache and no longer seared through him like a red-hot lance. He moved away, needing time to think, aware he had left out a huge chunk of important information but not yet ready to tell Polly what Elaine had done, or of his feelings, his guilt, concerned she would think badly of him. As he did of himself. Turning round, he discovered Polly hadn't moved, but was watching him through big blue eyes. There was no pity in their depths, but he saw sorrow, pain on his behalf, and the kind of empathy that inspired such confidence and trust from her patients.

Closing the gap between them again, he continued with the edited version of his tale. 'Suddenly I was left alone with newborn twins. And while grieving for Elaine, I somehow had to make important decisions about what to do.'

'It must have been impossibly difficult—a time of very mixed emotions.'

'Yes, it was,' he admitted, finding Polly as easy to talk to as he'd expected, and grateful that she faced things head on. 'I couldn't right the wrongs of the past, but I knew things had to change if I was to be any kind of father to Rosie and Toni. There were people who said I should give the girls up for adoption.'

'What nonsense. How could anyone suggest something like that?' she asked with evident disbelief and anger.

Luca was warmed by her support, amused by her fierce indignation, and alerted by a brief yet unmistakable flash of intense, dark pain. Puzzled, he filed the moment away for later. 'I don't know, but adoption was never an option.'

'Of course not.' Her voice was throaty with emotion, tightening his gut and firing his blood, but again he noted the underlying pain. 'How did you cope?'

'I had no close family in Italy by then. My only grandparent died when I was eleven, and my parents, who spent long periods of time working abroad, died when I was sixteen. But Elaine's parents were wonderfully supportive, and not just to the girls. Jane and Brian were like a second mother and father to me,' he confided, smiling as he thought of his in-laws.

'They were in Cornwall?'

'That's right.' In response to Polly's soft query, he explained how he had met Elaine when she had been backpacking in Italy during her gap year, and how they had fallen in love, changing the course of both their lives. 'We lived in Cornwall for a while, and I did some of my early training at St Piran's, but there came a point when Elaine and I decided to move back to Italy.'

Once more Luca hesitated. He didn't want to play what-if games in his head for the umpteenth time and wonder if Elaine would still be alive today if they had remained in Cornwall. Or if, at any point during those years, Elaine would have told the truth about the risk of what they were doing, and if he could have made her stop. If he had, of course, he would never have had the twins. Familiar guilt ripped at his heart. No man should have to make a choice between the lives of his wife and his children. Elaine had made the decision for him, driven by her single-minded determination—yet the consequences had been like playing Russian roulette with her life and those of the twins.

Elaine had paid the ultimate price. And he had lost the wife he loved. But he had gained their twins…her final gift to him. He'd wanted Elaine back, but how could he wish away his daughters? It had been an impossible situation, one that even now he had not properly resolved in his head. All he did know was that he didn't blame the girls or resent their existence, even though there had been moments of anger at Elaine…and himself. An unsteady breath shuddered through him.

'Luca, what is it?'

The whispered words and the light touch of Polly's fingers on his wrist brought him back with a start. Before she could move away, he captured her hand, needing her touch, the comfort of human contact. For a moment he looked at the contrast of her pale skin against his darker tones, entranced by the impossible fragility in the bones of her slender hand and graceful fingers. His gaze slowly trailed up over her floaty skirt—which today was a swirl of greens and blues—and over the now familiar layers of assorted tops she wore and which so effectively masked her body.

That brought him up short and for a moment he frowned, wondering why the fact that Polly was in hiding had not occurred to him before. Now that it had, he couldn't shake the thought. And when he saw the jumble of emotions chasing across her eyes, he knew he was right. He'd been aware of her heightened emotions at various times during the week, most especially with Kate, and yesterday at the school, when he had been uncertain of their cause but had welcomed her acceptance of his efforts of support. Now, though, he saw so much more. He saw the pain that raged inside her. A pain that might stem from a very different cause—and why/how/who/what/when questions raged in his mind—but that appeared as deeply ingrained as his own. Maybe it was one of the reasons they were so drawn to each other…one lost soul instinctively recognised and reached out to another.

'Luca?'

This time Polly's voice was laced with wary uncertainty, enough for him to refocus on what he had been saying but not enough for him to relinquish her hand when she tried to withdraw it. He could deny it and fight it all he wanted, but Polly set him on fire and his flesh burned from the contact with hers.

'Jane and Brian brought me and the girls back to Cornwall.' He cleared his throat, needing to finish the story before he could turn to other things. 'I finished my training at St Piran's, and they cared for the girls while I was at work. If I had continued with paediatric surgery, it would have entailed long shifts, spells of night duty and a lot of weekends, but I knew I needed a more settled routine and to work better hours if I was to have more time to be a father to my daughters, so I switched to general practice, which offered what I needed.'

He was aware of Polly searching his own expressions and he tried to keep himself open to her, wanting her to trust him the same way. 'Do you miss the surgery?'

Another kick-in-the-gut question. 'Sometimes, yes. But I genuinely enjoy being a GP,' he confided truthfully. 'Brian and Jane were both in their early seventies when the twins were born—Elaine was a late, unexpected but longed-for child after previous miscarriages and health problems.' Problems Elaine had inherited and which, combined with others, had led to the fatal complications with the twins—facts she hadn't shared with him until too late. He cleared his throat and pressed on. 'Brian and Jane became ever more frail and found it impossible to care for two active, growing girls. I arranged other help, not entirely successful, then this post came up. It was time for a change, for me to take responsibility for raising my daughters, and for Jane and Brian to relax.'

The older couple had a lot of medical issues between them and Luca was very concerned about them. He'd been relieved by their decision to move to a flat in a warden-assisted, sheltered-housing complex along the coast from Penhally.

'The girls must miss them,' Polly murmured, echoing his thoughts.

'They do. It was a big change in routine for them. We see them often, although their failing health means not for too long each time. Rosie and Toni can be frighteningly intuitive for such tiny tots.'

As he finished, he noted Polly's increased tension and emotional distance when he talked of his daughters. Why? It was the question that seemed to crop up most often with Polly. The more he learned about her, the less he seemed to know.

He hadn't so much as looked at another woman from the

moment he'd set eyes on Elaine twelve years ago, and that he not just noticed but was so attracted to Polly felt like a betrayal of the wife he had loved. His emotions and his libido had died with Elaine. He hadn't imagined them ever coming back to life. Apparently they'd only been in hibernation because his body responded in a once-familiar way to Polly, his interest and attraction increasing every day.

Why Polly? Why now? And what was he going to do about it?

Polly remained an intriguing and complicated puzzle, more and more difficult to solve and understand. As he watched her, she bit her lip, her gaze still averted following his mention of the twins, and his free hand moved with a will of its own, tipping up her chin before his fingers brushed her cheek. Even though his other hand was still holding hers, the instant his fingers made contact with her face it felt as if he had been plugged into an electric socket, so intense was the physical charge that shot through him.

Blue eyes widened in surprise but he also saw the answering awareness she failed to mask. Anxiety and confusion were evident, too, and gave him pause. Even white teeth nervously nibbled the soft swell of her lower lip, firing his blood and driving him insane. His thumb traced the outline of her upper lip, with its cute Cupid's bow, before teasing across the lower one, erasing the tiny indentations left by her teeth.

He heard her breath hitch and felt the racing of her pulse in her wrist. Her pounding heartbeat matched his own. This was crazy, and he knew it. If anyone had told him a week ago that he'd be lusting after and feeling protective of any woman, let alone one so opposite from Elaine, he would have considered having them certified. But Polly, his unique and fragile little gypsy, had thrown his life and his mind into total disarray, burrowing under his skin and refusing to be whittled out again.

'You were married once, too?' he ventured after a moment's silence, needing a few answers of his own.

'Yes.'

He barely heard her, so soft was her voice, but he registered the hurt that clouded her eyes and dulled their light. Again the pad of his thumb explored the succulent temptation of her lower lip. 'What happened, Polly?'

She shook her head, and long, dusky lashes lowered to hide her expression. Luca curbed his frustration, eager to uncover all her mysteries but scared of pushing too much too soon. A while ago he would never have imagined making this much progress with her. But he was desperate to know why Polly and her husband had divorced…and whether she was still in love with the man. That thought brought an uncomfortable burn far too reminiscent of jealousy.

'We've both had to adapt and cope, haven't we, *zingarella*?' he whispered, leaning closer, breathing in the delicious scent of lilacs, feeling the tremor that rippled through her. It took every scrap of self-restraint not to close the last of the distance and kiss her but it was too soon—for both of them. 'Sometimes life throws us unexpected challenges, no?'

Luca was startled by Polly's sudden humourless laugh. 'What a masterful understatement, Luca.'

The touch of uncharacteristic sarcasm was overridden by the raw emotions in her voice that conveyed not only agreement but also regret and a soul-deep pain that shook him to the core. Yet as he cupped her face, savouring the downy softness of her skin, concern for her was rivalled by the growing temptation that challenged the resolution he had made only moments ago not to kiss her.

'Talk to me,' he encouraged, hoping she could start opening up to him.

She shook her head. 'I can't.'

'Polly, I—'

To his intense frustration, the emergency bell sounded at the front door. He wanted more time alone with Polly, but the possibility that someone was in need could not be ignored. The bell rang again, and he cursed. Sighing, he stroked her face one last time, lost in the turmoil swirling in her eyes, then he allowed himself the briefest, lightest of kisses…brushing her lips with his own, getting the tiniest, most tantalising hint of her taste, whetting his appetite and leaving him craving more.

'This isn't finished, *zingarella*,' he whispered as he stepped back, reluctantly releasing her, his hands dropping to his sides as the bell rang a third time.

Aware of Polly's confusion, feeling as mixed up as she was, he forced himself to turn away and leave the room before he did something crazy—like throw all caution and common sense to the wind, gather her slender frame up in his arms, kiss her senseless and set them both on fire.

Left alone, and with her legs unable to hold her up a moment longer, Polly sank down, grateful there was a chair behind her. The information leaflets she'd been holding slipped from her nerveless fingers and scattered across the floor. Luca had been going to kiss her. Which was scary enough. More frightening still was that she had wanted him to…and was disappointed that he hadn't.

She had learned much more about him—about his wife, his loss, his daughters, and the changes he had made to his life to give the little girls the best he could. His pain had been evident and had twisted her heart. It had taken every bit of strength she possessed not to give in to her instinct to hug him. She was vulnerable to him and that made him dangerous, but keeping her distance, as she knew she must, was becoming harder with each passing day.

Luca's questions about her own marriage had caught her off guard. She never liked to think about Charles. Not for any reason. Kate was the only person who knew anything about what had happened, and even then Polly had been very careful to edit and censor her story, so the sudden compulsion she had experienced to confide in Luca had rocked her to the core. The thought of Luca knowing about her life, her mistakes, her marriage and what she had done, sent a chill down her spine. And the very fact that it mattered what he thought of her, and that she was even thinking like this, brought home how far he had broken through her defences in six days. Defences she had worked so hard to build since she had finally managed to put Charles behind her.

To this day she didn't know how something that had started out with such promise could have gone so badly wrong. She had believed in her marriage vows and had meant every word, including 'for better, for worse'. But that had been before she'd known what 'worse' was. Or that sometimes there came a point where you had to think of yourself, to recognise that however hard you try, other people have to take responsibility for their own actions and decisions, and there was nothing more you can do for them. All that was left was to survive…and to be safe, you have to walk away. By the time she had understood that and had reached that point with Charles, it had almost been too late, and the cost of doing it was more than she would ever have wanted to pay.

She had been living with the aftermath for nearly four years now. About three months longer than Luca had been living with his. Listening to him, she had heard his pain and anger and confusion, but also his love for his daughters, and she couldn't imagine how difficult it had been for him to have to try and reconcile gaining his children at the cost of his wife's life.

Hurting, for him and for herself, she slipped off the chair and knelt on the floor to begin gathering up the scattered leaflets, finding that her hands were still shaking in reaction. Distracted, she sat back on her heels, her fingers touching lips that still tingled from softest brush of his. Her eyes closed as she relived those few moments with Luca. She had been aroused by his subtle masculine scent and his gentle caresses, her whole body had been energised, her senses on high alert, and she had yearned for so much more.

Luca had said it wasn't finished, but it had to be. She couldn't allow anything else to happen, for many reasons. A sigh escaped as she tried to push her thoughts of Luca aside. Needing to return to her task if she was ever to finish up and escape for some time alone, Polly opened her eyes, smothering a gasp when she found herself looking at what had to be one of Luca's daughters. The little girl's dark brown eyes, so like her father's, were filled with curiosity. Dressed in a pretty red-and-white spotted dress, she stood a couple of feet away, silent and watchful, her silky dark hair cut into a bob that didn't quite reach her shoulders, her skin tone a shade or two lighter than Luca's.

Fearing that her heart was going to rip right out of her chest, Polly sucked in a steadying breath, completely unprepared for this moment. 'Hello. What's your name?' she finally managed, struggling not fall apart as pain washed through her.

'I'm Rosie.' The little girl stepped closer. 'Are you Polly?'

'Yes, that's right.' The realisation that Luca had spoken about her to his children added to her surprise and confusion.

Rosie's impish smile tightened the band around Polly's chest. 'You're Papà's friend.'

'We work together,' Polly murmured, her voice sounding rough as she tried to contain the emotions she feared might emerge if confronted with Luca's children.

Rosie tilted her head, an endearing little moue of consideration on her face. Despite herself, Polly couldn't help but be amused and enchanted by this gorgeous child. It took considerable willpower to resist the instinct to invite Rosie into her arms for a hug. Experiencing a wave of desperation, unsure how long she could maintain her composure, Polly looked towards the door, hoping Luca would come and collect his little stray.

'Toni hurt her hand and Papà is trying to mend it,' Rosie told her.

'I'm sure your sister will be fine.' Polly swallowed as the little girl edged closer until she could feel her pressing gently against her arm. 'Your Papà is a very good doctor.'

Rosie gave another sweet smile. 'He makes people better. Do you do that, too, Polly?'

'I try to.'

Apparently satisfied, Rosie nodded, leaning into her. 'What are you doing?'

'I dropped these leaflets on the floor and now I have to tidy them up. Do you want to help me?' she asked.

'OK.'

Rosie knelt down beside her and reached for one of the leaflets. Then another. Side by side they worked together in silence for a few moments and Polly would have laughed at the incongruity of it had she not been so on edge.

'Rosie?' Luca called from further down the corridor.

A lump lodged in Polly's throat at the way girl's face lit up in response to the sound of her father's voice. 'Rosie's with me, Luca,' she managed, steeling herself for the customary jolt that always rocked her when she saw him.

He arrived in seconds, looking heart-stoppingly sexy. 'Sorry about that. Carol, the childminder, knew I was here and brought them along when Toni cut herself rather than try and dress it herself or wait for me to pick them up in half an hour or so.'

'That was sensible of her. It must be a relief to have found someone reliable,' Polly murmured, still feeling very unsure and discomfited.

'It is. Nick put me in touch with her,' he informed her. 'She looks after some of his grandchildren and works closely with the nursery school, so it was ideal.'

For a moment Polly's gaze lingered on his mouth, warmth stealing across her cheeks as she recalled their nearly-kiss, then she looked away, suffering another painful pang as she focused on the girl holding his hand.

Almost identical to Rosie in terms of facial features, Toni's cheeks were slightly thinner, while her hair was an inch or so shorter. She was wearing jeans, trainers and a green sweat-shirt with animal pawprints on it, and her free hand sported a neat bandage.

'And how is Toni?' Polly was moved to ask as Luca let go of the little girl's hand and she skipped across to join her sister.

'She's fine…thankfully. The cut on the heel of her hand just needed cleaning and gluing.' His caring, benevolent smile as he moved close to his daughters and reached out to ruffle Toni's hair stripped another layer from Polly's frozen heart. 'This one is always up to mischief, aren't you, *trottola*?'

As Toni grinned, unrepentant, Rosie tugged at his other hand, claiming his attention. 'I've been helping Polly, Papà.'

'So I see, *topolino*,' he praised, gently tweaking the little girl's nose and making her giggle.

Hearing his pet names for his children and seeing how wonderful he was with them only added to Polly's pain. For a moment her gaze clashed with his, and the speculative gleam in his dark eyes made her acutely uncomfortable. She had no idea what he was thinking, just as he could have no idea what she was feeling. And she hoped to keep it that way. She didn't want Luca to know.

'You've been a great help, Rosie.' Rising shakily to her feet, Polly took the leaflets the girl held out to her. 'Thank you.'

Adding the papers to her own, she crossed the room and filed them away with much less care than usual, driven only by a desperate need to be alone to lick her wounds.

All week she had worked hard to keep Luca at a distance, and not to talk about, see pictures of or meet his children. She had sensed at once that he was dangerous to her but she had failed miserably at protecting her fragile heart. Now, what she had feared all along had happened. She was drawn to Rosie and Toni with as much need and yearning as she was to their father, but it was an impossible dream.

With unsteady fingers she fumbled with the key as she unlocked the desk drawer and took out her bag. Turning round, she saw the smiles on two adorable little faces, and then the puzzlement, concern and contemplation in Luca's eyes. There, right before her, was everything she had wanted but would never now have. A good man. Lovely children. Fixing an over-bright smile on her face, she edged towards the door.

'I'll leave you to lock up if that's OK,' she murmured, unable to meet Luca's gaze again.

Disappointed protests came from both girls, surprising her and bringing the threat of tears.

'Do you have to go?' Luca queried.

Backing up as he took a couple of steps towards her, Polly nodded, hoping her desperation didn't show in her voice. 'Yes.'

As she turned once more for the door, a tug on her skirt detained her and she looked down, finding Rosie beaming up at her. Confused, she hesitated, then Rosie beckoned for her to bend down. Polly did so, only for the little girl to shock her once again.

'Bye, Polly,' she whispered, pressing a kiss to her cheek.

Polly felt the burn of emotion at the back of her throat.

'Bye.' It was the only word she could manage and even then it sounded strangled.

She took a last look back at the special little family who had so swiftly and devastatingly breached her defences, then she fled. It hurt so much to remember, to think, to wonder how like Luca's two beautiful little girls her own daughter might have been. She would be the exact age of Rosie and Toni now…had she lived.

CHAPTER FIVE

'THE girls—especially Rosie—seem very taken with Polly. Who is she?' Jane Watson asked.

Sitting opposite his mother-in-law, and subjected to her direct green gaze, Luca felt himself blushing like a schoolboy, the mention of Polly's name sparking off an array of conflicting reactions. 'She's one of the doctors in Penhally.'

'And you like her?'

'I like all my new colleagues,' he responded, hoping the basic truth of his answer would mask his deeper confusion about Polly.

Jane chuckled. 'Luca!'

'I don't know. No. Yes.' Luca sighed, dragging a hand through his hair in exasperation. 'Look, I've only known her a week.'

'You and Elaine were certain of your feelings within hours of meeting,' Jane pointed out with maddening calm.

'This is a completely different situation. And Polly is nothing like Elaine,' he added, concerned how his in-laws might feel at the idea of another woman attracting his attention.

'And that's a good thing.' Leaning forward, Jane laid a hand on his arm and smiled. 'It shows you're ready and this might be real.'

Luca frowned. 'How do you mean?'

'Because you're not looking for someone like Elaine, trying to conjure up a substitute,' she explained.

'I'm not looking for anyone,' Luca insisted, troubled about the situation with Polly. 'There was only one Elaine.'

'I know, my love.' Jane's smile was tinged with sadness, and Luca followed her gaze as she looked at the photograph of Elaine on the mantelpiece.

Elaine and Polly were different in every way. He didn't want a replacement. He hadn't thought he wanted *anyone*, but a week with Polly and he was being forced to rethink everything. Not that he felt he knew her much better than on the day they had met, and he had yet to figure out her puzzling behaviour the previous afternoon.

'Brian and I hoped this would happen long ago,' Jane said, shocking him. 'You're a very attractive man, Luca, and an exceptionally good one. You have to start thinking about your needs.'

He hadn't had any needs. Not for a very long time. The only thing he had cared about was the twins, ensuring they grew up feeling secure and loved.

'Elaine wouldn't have wanted you to be alone, Luca. You have our blessing. And you aren't betraying Elaine, or letting anyone down.' She took his hand, green eyes moist with unshed tears, her words making him choke up with emotion. 'We know how much you loved Elaine. Nothing is going to take that away.'

Luca thought about Elaine's obsessive need for a baby, of her persistence, her furtiveness and odd behaviour when she became pregnant. 'I should have done something, should have seen.'

'Elaine should never have deceived you, Luca. You know how strong-willed she was. Even as a child, when she set her mind to something, there was no reasoning with her, no diverting her from the course she had set herself on.'

'I know, but…' He broke off, shaking his head, finding it difficult to set aside the guilt—and flicker of hurt, angry betrayal—that had weighed him down for so long.

Jane's fingers tightened on his. 'Luca, it is *not* your fault. No one blames you. *No one.* It's long past time you stopped blaming yourself and moved on with your life, not only for your sake but the girls' too. They need their father to be happy. And there will come a time in their lives when, no matter how marvellous you are, they'll need a woman's understanding.'

Maybe Jane was right, but he was confused, uncertain. Polly was so different from anyone he had ever known or been attracted to before. How did he know it was real? It wasn't as if Polly's life was uncomplicated. With each day that went by, and with each new scrap of information he unearthed about her, the more mysterious she became. And she seemed to have more baggage from her past than he did. He shook his head thinking of her rushed exit from the surgery yesterday and of Rosie's words after Polly had gone.

'What is it?' Jane asked, a quizzical smile on her face.

'I was just thinking of Rosie and how frighteningly perceptive she is—and she isn't four yet.'

Jane chuckled. 'Rosie has Elaine's intelligence, sensitivity and intuition, while Toni has her mother's energy, and her love of sport and adventure.'

'And for getting into trouble,' Luca pointed out, and they enjoyed a moment of shared laughter, thinking of the scrapes Toni had landed herself in. He didn't want to imagine what might lie ahead as she grew older. As for her sister… 'Rosie asked me why Polly is so sad inside. How can she see that at her age?'

'And is she right?' Jane queried.

'Yes.' That was one thing he *did* know. 'But I don't yet know why.'

Jane looked interested. 'Is she a local girl?'

'She is. Or was,' he amended.

'How do you mean?'

'She grew up in Penhally but left thirteen years ago,' he explained, drawing on the bits of information he had managed to glean. 'Her godmother and good friend persuaded her to take the GP job. Polly came back in July but I don't think she is finding the return to Penhally easy.'

Jane nodded. 'I suppose it depends why she left. If she has bad memories. What's her surname?'

'Carrick. At least, that's the name she's using now. It was her mother's maiden name. She died when Polly was young,' he confided, remembering the conversation he had overheard between Polly and Kate in the car.

'Carrick? Carrick…' Jane's eyes widened. 'Goodness, I wonder if it could be.'

Luca frowned. 'Could be what?'

'Do you know her father's name? Her mother's married name?'

'Reg Searle, I think,' Luca replied.

'Well!' Releasing his hand, Jane sat back in her chair and let out a rush of breath.

'Jane?'

She pressed her palms to her cheeks, a far-away look in her eyes for a moment. 'Yvonne Carrick. I used to teach her at school. I remember the gossip when Yvonne became involved with Reg Searle. We moved to St Piran because of Brian's job, and I gave up work to have Elaine, but I remember Yvonne died when her own child was very young.' She paused a moment and frowned. 'I have a hazy recollection that Penhally's formidable headmistress, Gertrude Stanbury, was concerned about the girl. That would be your Polly.'

His Polly... A riot of conflicting emotions churned inside him. What Jane had told him had been interesting, but there was little that helped him work out anything about Polly's life *now*. Whatever had happened in Polly's past had been sufficiently serious and important that it had had an impact on her present...and, unless he did something to stop it, it threatened her future, too. He had no idea what to do or how he could make a difference, he only knew he had to try.

All of which made a mockery of his resolution *not* to get involved with Polly and confirmed how far she had burrowed under his skin and into his heart in just one week. And all with no intent on her part. He knew Polly was as reluctant as he was to acknowledge the attraction between them and was fighting equally hard to stop it happening. He could tell her it was too late. The battle was over...he'd lost. And yet, instead of defeat, what he felt was a mix of trepidation, puzzlement, fear and a spine-tingling excitement.

His talk with Jane had given him a lot to think about, Luca admitted, but there was no time for more now as Brian arrived back at the small, ground-floor flat, having taken the twins to feed the fish in the pond in the centre of the communal garden belonging to the sheltered-housing complex. Brian, his thinning hair now almost white, leaned heavily on his walking stick, and he was breathing heavily when he sank into his armchair.

Luca glanced at his watch, surprised at the time. They had to get moving. After rounding up the twins and making sure they had everything, they said their goodbyes.

'Think on what I said, my love,' Jane whispered as she hugged him.

'I will. Thank you.'

Further delays ensued when Rosie discovered she had mislaid her favourite cuddly toy, and it was several moments before Pooh Bear was back in her arms.

'Come on, *bambine*,' Luca encouraged, hustling them out to the car. 'Or we'll be late for the beach picnic.'

'Papà, will Polly be there?' Rosie asked once they were on their way back along the coast.

The query took him by surprise. 'I don't know, *topolino*.'

'I hope so,' Rosie countered.

Never liking to be left out, Toni added her agreement. 'I want to see Polly, too.'

From the time they had been babies, the girls had proved to be remarkable judges of people, clear about who they liked and who they didn't, and he'd never known them to be wrong. But even he was surprised at the speed with which they had taken to Polly.

If Polly had been invited, would she go? One of the things he had learned during the week was how she generally kept to herself. The thought of seeing her brought excitement, doubt, arousal and confusion, and there was no denying that his heart rate had kicked up or that the blood was flowing hot through his veins.

A few minutes more and he was parking off road near the quiet cove Oliver had directed him to. He helped the girls change into their beach things, everything taking twice as long because they were bouncing with excitement and impatience. When they had everything, Luca changed his own things, welcoming the kiss of the September sun on his skin, then he picked up the cooler and locked the car.

There was no sign of Polly's little Renault and the sting of disappointment was acute. Of course, she might have come with some of the others, he reasoned. And the unanswered question about whether she was there or not had him quickening his pace as he led the girls down the steps carved into the rocks to the safe, sandy beach below.

'The forecast for Sunday is wonderful, so we're going to get together to relax and have fun,' Lauren had explained in the staffroom on Friday.

'You can swim or play ball,' Chloe had continued. 'Or you can read, have a nap, or just sit and talk and eat. Please come, Polly. We'll stop by on Sunday morning and pick you up.'

Although she usually went out of her way to avoid social gatherings, Polly had woken on Sunday morning to find herself anticipating the promised arrival of her new friends with eagerness. She had even braved the kitchen to make some muffins and cookies as her contribution to the picnic. Chloe and Lauren had seemed genuinely delighted, and their pleasure that she had chosen to accompany them for the day had given Polly a boost. As had the enthusiastic welcome she had received from Oliver and Gabriel—and Foxy the grey-hound—when she had climbed into the car.

A couple of hours had passed since then, and Polly had started to relax, largely thanks to the way her new friends had included her and set her at ease. They had talked about all sorts of things—and she had learned with dismay about Lauren's diagnosis of retinitis pigmentosa earlier in the year which meant she had to keep her sunglasses on to protect her eyes. There had been a lot of laughter and some gentle teasing, but Polly was grateful that none of them had pressed her to talk about herself.

Polly had been content to be left with her book while the others had gone for a swim. Now she sat on a blanket spread on the soft sand in the secluded cove a short distance along the coast from Penhally's busy main beach. It was a glorious day, the sun was shining and they pretty much had the small

cove to themselves. Setting her book aside, she wrapped her
arms around her drawn-up knees, smiling as she watched her
companions kick a football around in the shallows to the
eager delight of Foxy who bounded around them. Her smile
turned wry as she realised that here she was, thirty years old,
back in Penhally, and still sitting on the sidelines, keeping
apart, just as she had in all the years growing up here.

She thought of Kate and longed to see her. The older
woman had undergone her final session of radiotherapy on
Friday, and Polly knew that Rob and the boys had planned
something special for them to do together this weekend in
celebration. Polly was delighted for Kate—both that the
ordeal of her treatment was over and that she had a new man
in her life after so many years alone—so she felt guilty for
the twinge of disappointment that, thanks to a turn of events
no one could have foreseen, there had been little opportunity
since her return in July to have a real heart-to-heart with Kate.
And, since their conversation on Thursday, Polly was also now
impatient to hear whatever it was Kate needed to tell her
about Nick Tremayne.

A prickle of envy trickled through her as she saw Oliver
sweep Chloe up in his arms and kiss her passionately, before
setting her back on her feet. As Chloe headed back towards
her, Oliver plunged into the sea for a swim. They were such a
special couple, as were Gabriel and Lauren, who continued to
play with Foxy for a few more moments before Gabriel kissed
Lauren with equal fervor, then ran into the sea to join Oliver.

Polly wondered what it felt like to be that loved, that
secure, and seeing two couples who undoubtedly shared the
real thing only served to make her realise that she had never
come near it. She had hoped she had found it with Charles,
but it had been an illusion, a painful mistake, and after all that
had happened she felt certain she would never be able to love

or trust again. With Chloe and Lauren approaching, she struggled to hide her feelings and shake off her introspection.

'I'm pooped.' Chloe laughed, briskly drying herself with a towel and wrapping a sarong around her waist and over her one-piece swimsuit before sitting on the blanket.

Pulling a T-shirt on over her bikini, Lauren knelt down, nodding her agreement. 'You definitely have the right idea, just chilling out, Polly.' Pulling out an old towel, she gave Foxy a quick rub.

'Oh, they're here!' Chloe exclaimed.

Lauren looked up from her task and adjusted her sunglasses. 'Great.'

Wondering what had caught her friends' attention, Polly looked over her shoulder and her mouth went dry. Luca! She had not known he'd been invited, too. For the moment she was too overwhelmed to think straight as her gaze locked on the sight of him wearing nothing but figure-hugging swim shorts. The black Lycra hung low on his hips, leaving his impressive torso bare, while the legs of the shorts moulded his legs to mid-thigh.

Polly's pulse started racing and she couldn't stop staring at him. Whereas both Oliver and Gabriel were gorgeous and both had lean, athletic bodies, she scarcely noticed them as they jogged up from the sea to meet the new arrival. Her gaze was riveted on Luca. He was a few inches shorter than the other two men and he was bigger built, less streamlined. But there wasn't an ounce of spare flesh on him. He was all muscle, solid and strong.

Luca had more hair on his chest than the other men, too. The flat, dark ruby-red orbs of his nipples nestled within the dark whorl of curls that spread across and between his pecs. The hair arrowed down in a dark line to his navel, continuing down over olive-toned skin to disappear beneath the low-slung waistband of his shorts. Her traitorous fingers itched to explore his body, to know the texture of his skin, the firmness of the muscles rippling beneath the smooth flesh.

The undeniable attraction and arousal Luca caused made her think of sex. And how long it had been since she had even been cuddled, let alone had felt loved—even if it had been an illusion. She pressed her palms to overheated cheeks. Her experience had been limited, Charles her only lover, but even with her hang-ups about her body, the physical side of their relationship had been nice…in the beginning.

When things had started to go wrong in other ways, so had their love-making, and when they had reached the point where Charles had no longer touched her at all, she had been relieved. She had shut that side of herself down ever since, more so for the last four years with the ending of her marriage and the loss of her baby.

She had never imagined wanting to be with another man again, to be held and kissed and touched and loved, especially as the issues with her body had increased, filling her with dread at the thought of anyone seeing her naked. But since meeting Luca, everything in her had reawakened and she felt edgy with desire and longing and unfulfilled need. There was no denying the fact that she ached with wanting him. But she couldn't have him. And not only because of her fears about her body. She wasn't a one-night-stand kind of woman, neither did she want to get involved again. Given his circumstances, she couldn't imagine that Luca did either. Far safer if she worked harder to fight against the attraction now, before she did anything foolish.

'Polly!'

Her name, called in high-pitched excitement, drew her attention away from Luca and for the first time she noticed the twins. As Rosie ducked out from behind her father and ran across the soft sand as fast as her little legs would carry her, a lump of emotion lodged in Polly's throat. She didn't want to bond with these children, but even though she had only met them once, she knew it might already be too late.

As Toni set off in hot pursuit of her sister, Rosie caught her foot on the edge of the blanket, a comical expression of surprise on her face as momentum propelled her small body towards Polly. And no matter how she told herself that she only opened her arms and caught Rosie because the little girl might have hurt herself with her ambitious flying leap, Polly knew it was a lie. Instinctively, she held the child against her, the feel of her and the scent of fruity shampoo and baby powder tugging at her heartstrings and twisting the pain inside her.

Giggling, Rosie wrapped her arms tightly around Polly's neck and planted a kiss on her cheek. Then, holding on with one arm, she looked towards her father and rapidly approaching sister with a triumphant grin on her face.

'Papà, I told you Polly would come,' she declared.

Toni, still with her bandaged hand, pushed her way in, determined to make room for herself on Polly's lap, and kissed her other cheek. 'Me, too.'

Polly struggled to choke back tears, her gaze inexorably lifting up the masculine length of Luca's body as he arrived at the blanket and set down the cooler and other things he was carrying. Then she met the watchful speculation and burn of fire in his dark eyes, and the aching knot of need and want tightened inside her. Scared at what was happening, she dropped her arms, thankful when the twins reluctantly moved away to be introduced to the others by their father.

'Rosa Jane and Antonia Elaine,' she heard, missing many of the words as she lost herself in the husky, sexy sound of Luca's voice.

'But everyone calls me Toni...'

'And me Rosie,' the girls explained in tandem.

Polly tensed as Luca knelt down on the blanket, far, far too close to her. Then her heart turned over with a mix of pain and longing as Luca sat back on his heels and gathered both girls into his arms, kissing them and tickling them until each was breathless from laughing.

Once released, the twins switched their attention to Foxy and, for a dog Lauren had told her was once people shy, the greyhound accepted the attention with remarkable fortitude.

'Why don't you all go and have another swim or play with the girls before lunch?' Polly suggested, needing a few moments to regather her composure. 'I'll set the things out and call you when it's ready.'

She was relieved when Oliver, Chloe, Gabriel and Lauren agreed without protest, taking the ball and moving down the beach with the girls and Foxy. Much to Polly's dismay, however, Luca remained behind, which was *not* what she had intended. Oh, help…she didn't want to be alone with him!

'Hello, Polly.'

Flustered by the throaty purr of his voice, positive he had moved even closer, she couldn't stop fidgeting—anything other than look at him or, worse, give in to the temptation to touch him. 'Hi,' she managed to reply, busying herself unpacking the picnic plates, cutlery and cups, before turning her attention to the food in the coolers.

'You don't want to swim yourself?' Luca asked, automatically helping her with the tasks.

She shook her head, her long plait bouncing against her shoulders. 'I'm not keen on the water.'

Her disobedient gaze flicked to him and she couldn't force it away again. She cursed the tinge of colour that warmed her cheeks in response to his nearness. For the first time she noticed the tattoo over his heart, above his left nipple, partially hidden beneath his chest hair, her attention lingering far too long as she deciphered the design. It was plain and simple but clearly heartfelt, and combined the names of his children in the shape of a cross and written in blue, with ANTONIA going across horizontally and ROSA going vertically, down through the central O.

'I had it done straight after they were born,' Luca told her, his voice rough with emotion. 'To keep them close to my heart and remind me they were my reason to go on living without Elaine.'

Any embarrassment she felt at being caught looking at him was washed away by the pain that ripped through her at his words. 'I'm sorry,' she whispered, unable to halt the single tear that spilled between her lashes and dropped onto her cheek.

'Don't cry for me, *zingarella*.'

The softness of his words was matched by the gentleness of his caress as he raised one hand, the pad of his thumb catching the tear and brushing it away. It sat for a moment, beaded on his skin. Then he raised it to his lips and sucked it inside his mouth, tasting her, the gesture so tiny but so erotic that Polly forgot how to breathe.

His palm cupped her face, and a shiver ran through her at the sensation of his touch. It was impossible to drag her gaze from his. She feared she would lose herself in those deep, dark eyes—eyes that saw into her very soul. As his thumb traced the swell of her lower lip, she could feel every rapid beat of her heart. His touch was unmistakably male, making her wonder how his hands would feel on the rest of her body and sending heat coursing through her.

A sudden shout and burst of laughter snapped her out of the spell of the moment, and she dragged a shaky breath into lungs that felt starved of oxygen as she drew away from Luca. She glanced round, thankful that no one was looking in their direction.

'You have beautiful children,' she murmured, her voice unsteady, returning to her task unpacking the lunch things in an effort to mask the way her hands were shaking. 'You've done a great job with them.'

Again Luca moved to help her. 'Thank you.'

'They look so alike and yet are very different,' she added, cursing the wistful edge that laced her words as her gaze strayed to watch Rosie and Toni playing…pain for what was lost and yearning for what would never be stealing through her.

'From the first they swiftly developed distinct personalities.' Luca sat back, a smile on his face as he watched his daughters, tightening the ache inside her even further. 'Rosie is a thinker. She is quiet and very sensitive. Toni's a doer, confident, always jumping in with both feet. Rosie is frighteningly intelligent, and learns easily, while Toni is sporty, a tomboy, fearless and keen to try everything.' He gestured to the first-aid kit he had brought. 'That's nothing to do with being a doctor, that's knowing we can rarely go anywhere without Toni getting into some scrape or another.'

'You have nicknames for them…what do they mean?'

Luca chuckled, and the sound seemed to vibrate down her spine, making her tingle. 'Rosie, quiet but also very inquisitive, became *topolino*, or little mouse. Toni, always on the go and often leaving chaos in her wake, became *trottola*, meaning spinning top or, sometimes *terremoto*—earthquake,' he explained, the love and affection so clear in his voice squeezing her heart.

Polly smiled, touched by his love for the girls and interested in his insight about their individual characters, probably the reason he never seemed to dress them in copycat outfits. He looked horrified when she said as much.

'Never. They aren't toys or clones of each other. Each has

her own taste. Occasionally they'll pick the same thing, usually in a different colour, but less often the older they get.'

'What about hobbies?' she asked, taking the muffins and cookies she had made out of her bag and adding them to the spread, automatically taking the wallet and keys Luca handed her for safekeeping and zipping them into a pocket in her canvas bag.

Luca leaned back on one elbow, half-turned towards her, and she struggled not to stare at his impressive physique— again. 'Rosie likes her soft toys, dressing up and anything to do with fairies! Toni is good with her hands and likes being on the go outside. Sometimes there's a squabble, but they get on well. And they're both mischievous. I wanted them to know their Italian heritage, so they've been bilingual from the outset. But it can cause problems,' he admitted with a heart-stoppingly sexy chuckle that lodged the breath in her chest.

'How come?'

'They quickly learned they can speak Italian to each other and most people can't understand. I try to stop them doing it. And it's very embarrassing if they say something cheeky to a teacher—especially if the person *does* understand!' he confessed, making her laugh. 'Together, they have a lot of interests they share…a love of books, Disney films, dancing and, most especially, animals. In fact—'

He broke off, his gaze returning to the girls as they played with Foxy. 'What?' Polly prompted, watching them, too.

'They've been pestering me about a dog. I'm weakening.' He sighed and shook his head, his smile wry. 'They can wrap me round their little fingers!'

Polly sighed, too, the knot of pain fisting inside her as her gaze was drawn inexorably to the two small girls running and laughing on the sand. She was unable to watch them without thinking about her own lost daughter. Would she have been advanced for her age, outgoing and adventurous like Toni, or thoughtful and sensitive like Rosie? She jumped as Luca caught her chin and turned her to face him.

'Why does looking at my children make you so sad, *zingarella*?'

Polly could only stare at him in stunned disbelief, affected by the soft huskiness of his words and by his scary insight. She shook her head, panic rising inside her. She wasn't ready to talk about it—wasn't sure she ever would be. But…

Thankfully, she was saved from answering as a warning shout alerted them to a miskick that sent the football sailing through the air over their heads. Foxy came charging by, missing the picnic food but bumping into Polly, knocking her off balance and toppling her into Luca. He caught her, strong arms wrapping protectively around her, and Polly experienced several moments of suspended animation, the world around them fading away, all her awareness centred on Luca. His heady, sexy scent teased her nostrils. Her traitorous fingers lingered, assessing and savouring the textures of smooth warm skin, firm muscles and the surprisingly soft dark hair on his chest.

The overriding impression was of strength, of maleness and of intense sexual longing as the customary electricity arced between them. Unfathomable dark eyes looked into hers and she feared he would read her reaction to him and recognise her body's desire. Embarrassed, she tried to push away, but it seemed ages before Luca finally loosened his hold. He helped her upright but still didn't release her, his hands moving from her shoulders to glide down her back.

'Are you all right?'

The sultry, intimate tone of his voice played havoc with her resolve, but somehow Polly nodded. 'I'm fine. It was nothing.' Which was a monstrous lie.

She was supremely conscious of his touch, which branded her even through her clothes. Her body was pressed against his, and while she never wanted to move, she knew she had to. She was scared—of so many things. And this couldn't happen. She couldn't let it. Again she made an effort to withdraw from him, grateful when the twins came running up, closely followed by the adults, everyone talking, apologising and laughing at once, and checking she was OK.

Polly sensed Luca's frustration and heard his soft curse as she shifted to put some distance between them.

'No damage done,' Polly reassured them, her smile over-bright.

As everyone sat down, eager to satisfy the hunger they had worked up for lunch, Polly could only think of a different kind of hunger…her own for Luca. A hunger she feared would continue to grow and which she could never risk assuaging.

CHAPTER SIX

'Oh, Polly, these lime and coconut muffins are to die for,' Chloe enthused, a smile of bliss on her face. 'How much will it cost me to bribe you to give me the recipe?'

'I'll write it out for you…free of charge!'

Luca heard Polly's soft, shy reply. Her ash-blonde hair was drawn up and secured in a knot, leaving her face and neck exposed, highlighting her exquisite bone structure and revealing the colour that bloomed on her pale cheeks in response to Chloe's compliment.

He'd noticed a lot of things about Polly during the picnic lunch. To begin with, the twins had taken most of his attention, but once they had decided what they wanted and had settled to eat their food, he had been able to switch his focus back to Polly.

That's when he'd realised what Polly was doing.

In the self-appointed role of waitress, passing round the various foods everyone had contributed and refilling the plastic mugs with fruit smoothie, lemonade or water, she was cleverly keeping everyone else happy and too busy to notice that she wasn't eating anything herself. It was subtle but obvious if you studied her. And he did. Polly picked at things…a bit of salad, a sliver of chicken or some of the delicious blue cheese which Chloe, who claimed to be addicted to it, told him came from the Trevellyans' farm shop. He'd made a mental note to buy some. But Polly, by always having something in her hand, and switching her attention between different people, masked the fact that she never actually put any food in her mouth.

Looking up, he met Oliver's gaze and saw the concern in his new friend's eyes. In the week he'd been at the surgery, Luca had discovered that Oliver was not only an exceptional doctor but very empathetic and aware of people. Now Luca shared with him a moment of silent understanding. Oliver had noticed too.

A frown knotted his brow as he thought back over the days he'd spent with her. He'd never seen her eating. She had made herself scarce at lunchtime, and on the day she had claimed to have eaten at her desk—when Nick had taken him to Smugglers for lunch—Luca had seen no evidence of it when he'd returned. The only thing she consumed at work was that insipid-looking cranberry-flavoured white tea.

Then there were her clothes. It had occurred to him the previous afternoon that Polly was hiding herself. Today was no exception. While everyone else wore bathing suits or shorts and T-shirts, Polly was wrapped up in an over-sized, albeit colourful gypsy skirt and layers of tops. The only difference was that now her feet were bare. A lump lodged in his throat. They were small, pale and delicate, and his gaze lingered as he noted that today her neatly groomed nails were painted pastel pink. *Dio!* He definitely had a thing about her toes.

With difficulty, Luca forced himself to return to the matter at hand and face the worrisome possibility that Polly had issues about her body and, maybe, about food, too. He'd seen from first meeting her that she was absurdly slender. Too slender? When she had fallen into him and he'd been able to hold her close for far too short a time, there had been nothing of her! More pieces of the Polly jigsaw were slotting into place but he wasn't close to seeing the whole picture, and he had ever more questions that needed answers.

This time last week, the furthest thing from his mind had been any kind of involvement with a woman. Then he'd met Polly. And now he couldn't get her out of his head, or stop his body responding every time he was close to her, or heard her voice, or breathed in her lilac scent, or thought of her. Which seemed to be all the time. Something indefinable about Polly Carrick, his little gypsy, called to everything in him and, quite without knowing it, she was reawakening parts of him that had shut down when Elaine had died. And for the first time in nearly four years, something other than his children and, to a lesser extent, his job mattered to him.

'Your girls look so cute.' Lauren's comment—as she helped herself to the rapidly dwindling stock of Polly's home-made white chocolate and raspberry cookies—caught Luca's attention. 'They had the time of their lives with Foxy. I think the three of them wore themselves out!'

Dragging his gaze away from Polly and looking at Rosie and Toni, Luca's heart swelled with love for them. They had started wilting part-way through their picnic lunch and were now curled up together, sound asleep. Foxy lay as close as possible, his head on his paws as he watched over them.

'Make the most of the lull. I know from experience they'll wake with batteries recharged and will be up and running again,' he replied with a wry smile, making his companions chuckle.

As if drawn by some invisible magnetic pull, Luca's gaze returned to Polly. Her lips were curved but her half-smile bore evidence of the same sadness he saw in her eyes when-ever she watched his daughters. He'd witnessed it several times…enough to suspect that the awkwardness she displayed around young children was nothing to do with disliking them and everything to do with the shadows of pain and longing in her eyes when she saw them.

Much to his frustration, they'd been interrupted earlier and he hadn't been able to get an answer from Polly about her reaction to the girls, but there was no doubt his question had rattled her. Had she wanted a baby and, for some reason, her husband had not? Was that why her marriage had failed?

'Did you talk to Dragan about the puppies?'

Oliver's query snapped Luca from his latest thoughts about Polly. 'Yes, and he's almost convinced me! When I foolishly promised the girls a dog once we had moved and settled in, I meant in a couple of years, not months, and I was thinking more of a rescue dog, older and trained already.' He glanced again at his sleeping daughters. 'Their grandparents' dog died six months ago and they miss him. I'm just concerned whether a puppy is right for three-year-olds, and how we'd manage,' he admitted, interested to hear his new friends' views.

'Rosie and Toni are nearly four, Luca, and they definitely have an instinct with animals. They've been gentle and sensible with Foxy,' Gabriel pointed out.

'I agree.' Chloe leaned back against Oliver's chest, smiling as her husband wrapped her in his arms, and Luca pushed away a flicker of envy at their closeness. 'And as for any worries about managing, you'll never have another chance like this one for full doggy support!'

'How do you mean?' Luca asked, taking another cookie before they all vanished.

'I popped in to see the puppies yesterday—oh, they're so cute! Melinda said that only two of the six are left without definite homes, and one of those is on reserve. So far none of the puppies are leaving Penhally!' Chloe explained, green eyes sparkling with excitement.

Chuckling, Lauren took up the story. 'Dragan and Melinda are keeping one puppy, Kate is taking one for Jem, and Gabriel and I are having one as a companion for Foxy. Having been reassured about introducing a puppy to a home with cats, Oliver and Chloe are having the other one. So if Nick's niece Charlotte goes ahead and takes the one on reserve and you have the other one, we'll all be together!'

'We're going to have a puppy crèche! And aside from helping each other in the early weeks, we also have Melinda on hand for veterinary advice, and she's organising puppy training classes for all of us when the time comes,' Chloe told him.

Lauren sighed, a wistful look on her face, her hands lightly massaging Gabriel's scalp as he lay with his head in her lap. 'Another week, two at the most, and we'll know which pup is ours. I can't wait for that!'

'Or for mid-October when we can take them home,' Chloe added.

'Oh, Luca,' Lauren murmured, adjusting her sunglasses and looking again at the girls curled up with Foxy. 'You and the twins *have* to have one. And you live so close to the four of us it will be no bother to get together and help.'

'Flatcoats are excellent with children.' Oliver took a sip of his drink. 'We always had animals at home when I was growing up and I think pets are really good for children. Aside from the fun and companionship, an animal teaches them to be unselfish, to care for another life and be responsible for its needs, and, inevitably, it helps them to understand loss.'

It made sense, Luca admitted. And, as Chloe had said, when might he get an opportunity again to consider a puppy with such an excellent background and with so much support on hand from friends? Luca vowed to go and see Melinda and Dragan—and the puppies—as soon as possible. Maybe Polly would go with him.

'I was never allowed any pets when I was young,' Chloe told them, and Luca caught an edge in the her voice, noting how Oliver cuddled her closer and Lauren reached out to touch her hand. Clearly there was a story there.

'Neither was I.' Polly's words were soft and shaky. 'Although my mother had a dog when I was very young.'

Luca was immediately aware that everyone was looking at Polly in surprise. In the time he'd known her, Luca knew how rare it was for Polly to volunteer anything about her private self. A hush fell as everyone waited, willing her to continue. Luca shifted closer to Polly and, out of sight of the others, rested his hand on her back, trying to give silent support.

'His name was Barney,' Polly continued after a moment, her head turned away, her gaze focused, he was sure, not on the scene around them but on something far away in her past. 'I loved him. He was my only friend. And I clung to him when my mother died. But—'

Her words snapped off and Luca sensed the group holding a collective breath. He believed Polly needed to begin trusting the people who cared about her and to release whatever was bottled up inside. Before he could prompt her, Chloe, who was sitting on her other side, did it for him.

'What happened, Polly?' she asked gently, handing over a tissue, her smile understanding.

'My father never liked Barney—he hated anything that took attention away from him or that someone might like more than him.'

Concerned only for Polly, and uncaring if any of the others noticed, Luca took her hand and linked their fingers, trying to convey his understanding and encouragement.

'Of dubious parentage, Barney was nothing much to look at, but he was loyal and loving and just the friend I needed. He never left my side at home. About a week after my mother

died, I was brought home from nursery school to find that
Barney had gone.' Polly looked pale and fragile and, while her
voice was little more than a whisper, it was laden with remembered pain, confusion and distress. 'I cried and cried, unable
to understand. My father just laughed. Then he told me he'd
disposed of Barney. I didn't understand, just that the friend I
needed was gone and my father had taken pleasure in the fact
that I was upset and had lost something important to me. I
never found out if Barney had been put to sleep or given away
to a new home.'

As a shocked stillness fell over the group, Luca's fingers
instinctively tightened on Polly's and he tried to swallow the
lump in his throat, aching for the child she had been. Her
father's deliberate cruelty was inexcusable enough, but it was
his apparent enjoyment of it that appalled Luca and made him
as angry as hell. As he was struggling with his increasing
awareness of her and the growing desire to hold and comfort
her, to protect her, he had another disturbing realisation. The
sickening possibility that this could be but one example of her
father's cruelty. She had been left alone with the man from the
age of four. Just what had Polly's childhood really been like?

He didn't have long to ponder on the question of Polly's
past as the conversation moved on to the experiences others
had had with animals, and then Lauren turned back to him, a
mischievous glint in her grey eyes.

'You wait, Luca. Two little girls who love animals…it'll
be ponies next!' she teased him.

'They're way ahead of you, Lauren,' he countered with a
smile. 'The pleas for riding lessons have already started.'

He noted Lauren's gaze flick to Polly. 'Didn't you ride at
one time, Polly? I seem to remember you spent a lot of time
at the Somers' stables.'

'Um, yes.' Still holding Polly's hand, Luca not only felt the

tightening of her fingers around his but also sensed the growing tension within her, and his thumb strayed to the inside of
her wrist, picking up the quickening beat of her pulse. 'I went
up there sometimes and helped out with chores in exchange
for a ride.'

She'd told them the bare facts but Luca was convinced by
her tone and the responses he had detected from her that the
stables had been important to her. 'Have you ridden since,
Polly?' he asked, seeing myriad emotions reflected in her
eyes as she turned her head and met his gaze.

'On and off.' She bit her lip, a tinge of pink staining her
cheeks in evidence of some emotional discomfort. 'But not
in the last few years.'

'You'll have to visit the stables when you have time, Polly.
I'm sure Georgie would love to see you,' Lauren suggested,
smiling down at Gabriel.

'Georgie's still there?'

Luca heard surprise, curiosity, pleasure and a touch of anxiety in Polly's reply. Again her fingers clung to his, although
he wasn't sure if she was even aware of it as she sat with a
far-away look on her face.

'Very much so! Georgie's in charge there now her
parents have retired,' Lauren informed her in response to
Polly's question.

'Georgie got married eighteen months ago. Her husband
is a Romany,' Chloe added, with obvious affection. 'He's an
incredible horseman and really lovely.'

'Polly, why don't you take Luca and the girls out to the
stables and show them around? Georgie is the perfect person to
give the twins lessons,' Lauren suggested, and Luca wanted to
hug her for giving him an excuse to spend more time with Polly.

The woman in question was clearly startled by the suggestion if her 'Oh!' was any guide.

'I'd like that very much, Polly.' Luca met her blue gaze and pressed home his advantage. 'And the girls would be so thrilled.'

'Perhaps we can arrange something, then,' she murmured.

Feeling a twinge of guilt for tricking her into the situation, Luca brushed a soothing caress across her wrist over the point where her pulse beat a rapid tattoo. 'Thank you, *zingarella*.'

It was wonderful to just *be*. Kate inhaled a deep breath of clean air, content to sit enjoying the late September sunshine and the chrysanthemums, dahlias and other flowers that continued to give a splash of bright colour as summer slid languorously towards autumn. Since the end of her course of radiotherapy last Friday, she felt as if a weight had been lifted from her shoulders and, although still tired and uncharacteristically emotional, she felt relieved, more relaxed and, above all, *free*.

Kate patted the space beside her on the rustic bench in the rear garden of her cottage and beckoned Polly to join her. She had indulged in some uncharacteristic but gentle meddling since July, which she excused because she wanted Polly to be happy. Focused on battling breast cancer and unable to give Polly the support she deserved, Kate had felt justified in asking Oliver, Chloe, Gabriel and Lauren to watch over Polly, thankful when the friendships had grown naturally. Luca's recent arrival was an unexpected bonus and one Kate had shamelessly exploited when she had noticed the attraction between Polly and the new Italian doctor.

'How was the beach picnic on Sunday?' she asked, knowing the subjects of the puppies and the riding stables had been raised.

'It was good—everyone seemed to have fun.'

Kate glanced at Polly's finely etched profile. 'Including you?'

'Yes. I didn't think I would, but I did. I even made some muffins and cookies as my contribution to the food,' she added, her smile tinged with sadness. 'They're the only two recipes of my mother's I was able to salvage.'

Kate suppressed a shiver as she thought of all Polly had been through after Yvonne had died, leaving her alone from the age of four with Reg Searle. The man didn't deserve to be called Polly's father. It made Kate furiously angry but also weighed down with guilt because, despite all her efforts, she hadn't been able to do anything to get Polly away from the beastly man. Pushing the disturbing thoughts away, she concentrated on Polly and the here and now.

'And did you eat anything?' she asked softly, already knowing the answer.

Betraying colour warmed Polly's cheeks. 'I couldn't, Kate. But no one noticed.'

Kate didn't have the heart to tell her that both Luca and Oliver had been very aware that Polly had issues with food. A frown creased Kate's brow as she remembered when her beloved goddaughter had been eleven and had shown the first signs of anorexia, the disorder she would struggle with throughout her early teens. Already tiny for her age, she had shrunk before Kate's eyes. Gertrude Stanbury, then headmistress at Penhally High, had been concerned, too. They had tried hard to help but with Reg denying them access to Polly, and generally being obstructive, it hadn't been easy.

Polly's interest in ponies had done much to help her back then and Kate hoped revisiting the riding stables would enable Polly to deal with some of the issues from the past. Especially if Luca was with her in support. That the twins wanted riding lessons was a stroke of good fortune and provided another opportunity for Polly and Luca to be together. But that was for the future. For now her thoughts returned to the past.

By the time Polly had left Penhally, determined to escape Reg's control and to go to medical school, she had been physically well again. There had been a blip, a risk of her slipping back into the grips of anorexia again, when things had gone wrong in her marriage and with the events surrounding her losing her baby. Again she had pulled through and, while always svelte, she was healthy. Or so Kate had thought.

'Is there a problem here, Polly?' she asked now, voicing her concern, wishing once again that things had been different and she had been able to give Polly more time and support since her arrival.

'No.' Sapphire-blue eyes looked at her and Kate saw the truth in them. 'I was at risk of a relapse four years ago, but the counselling I had after losing the baby also helped get the anorexia back under control before it took hold again. Things have been much better, except…'

Kate slipped an arm around Polly's shoulders. 'Except?'

'I know it's stupid, but I still find it a struggle to eat in front of other people.'

'You eat in front of me,' Kate reminded her.

Polly's smile was sad. 'You know me. You've seen me at my worst and been there for me. Even now, all these years on, it's hard to ignore the voice in my head that tells me people are watching what I eat and judging me—and that I don't deserve to enjoy anything or to have nice things.'

'Oh, Polly,' Tears stung Kate's eyes as she hugged this special young woman.

'The rational part of me knows I should have overcome these feelings of inadequacy years ago, but they're so deeply ingrained.' She paused and bit her lip. 'In my head I'll always be Plain Polly from Penhally.'

'No!' Kate fought the fury that rose inside her at the damage Reg had done to his daughter with his verbal cruelty. 'Listen to me, my love. You are a beautiful, smart, funny, caring and wonderful woman—*that* is who people see.'

Polly shook her head and wiped a hand across her eyes, tears beading on her lashes. 'I hate my body. Sitting on the beach last Sunday, I felt so dowdy and unfeminine next to Chloe and Lauren, like a skinny runt. Luca was there…with his children—' She broke off and turned her head, allowing Kate to see the conflicting emotions warring in her eyes.

'Polly…'

'It hurts, Kate. I see girls the same age as my daughter would have been now and I can't help but wonder what she would have been like.' Kate felt her own heart constrict in response to Polly's pain. 'And as for Luca—'

'Before you start running yourself down again, young lady,' Kate interrupted, 'the charge of attraction zinging back and forth between you and Luca was obvious. And he looked more than interested in you!'

Polly shook her head, clearly agitated. 'Oh, Kate, I'm so confused. Any woman with half a breath left in her body would find him attractive. And his children are so beautiful. I've tried to keep myself at a distance from them all, but those girls…they just slipped right through my defences. And so did their father. But I'm *scared*, Kate,' she confided.

'I know, my love.'

Kate rested a comforting hand on the younger woman's back, her heart going out to her. Polly had been through so much, both as a child and with the awful end to her marriage—about which there was much Kate was sure she didn't know, believing Polly had kept the worst from her. She wanted Polly to move on, to be loved as she deserved, and from what Kate had seen and heard of Luca, she was hopeful he could be the right man to provide all Polly needed…including his daughters.

'I've resigned myself to never having children. And I swore I'd never get involved with anyone again,' Polly continued. 'I can't handle any more heartache, or finding myself back in a controlling situation again. I've made so many mistakes.'

'You are not to blame for anything, Polly,' Kate insisted firmly. 'Nothing that happened when you were growing up, or in your marriage, was your fault. *Nothing*. Please, my love, don't let Reg, or Charles, continue to influence your life.'

'How do you mean?' Polly asked with a puzzled frown.

'Coming back to Penhally was always going to be hard, and I'm so proud of you for doing it, not to mention overjoyed at having you close to me again,' she told her, briefly resting a hand against Polly's pale face. 'There are ghosts you need to lay to rest so that you can draw a line under the past and let it go.' Kate turned more to face Polly, needing to get through to her. 'If you shut yourself away from life, and from love, then Reg and Charles are still pulling the strings and controlling you. Don't let them win. Set yourself free. It's obvious that you and Luca have a connection. Give yourself a chance. Give Luca a chance. He could be the best thing that's ever happened to you.'

Polly drew in a ragged breath. 'I don't know.'

'It's understandable that you're scared. There's no need to rush into anything. A step at a time. Take Luca and the girls to the riding stables, spend time together. See what happens. And there are the puppies. You've been to see them, yes?' Kate asked, seeing the smile ease the worry from Polly's face.

'We went yesterday. They're so cute!' She laughed, wiping away a lingering tear. 'Luca's not telling the girls, he's going to surprise them when they go to pick the puppy up to take him home.'

Delighted to see Polly smiling again, Kate laughed. 'I know what you mean. Jem has wanted a puppy for ages. He's coped so well all summer while I was ill, and I feel he's earned it and is responsible enough to take care of an animal.'

Kate shook her head, pushing down her own emotions as she thought not just how wonderful her son had been but of what she still had to tell Polly about the real identity of Jem's father. 'I went with Rob and the boys to see the puppies and now I'm as excited as Jem! He's chosen his puppy, he even has a name…Bruno. And he and Matthew are busy getting everything ready from Melinda's list.'

Kate cherished this time with Polly but, aware the boys would soon be home from school, she knew she had to face things and confess her secret to Polly while they were still alone. A shiver went through her. How could she explain? She had betrayed James on the night he had died. With Nick. A ragged breath escaped her.

'Kate, what's wrong?' Polly asked, her dark blue eyes clouding with concern.

'I need to tell you something.' Her voice wobbled and a smile was impossible. 'Oh, God, this is so hard.'

She saw Polly's already pale face turn ashen. 'The cancer…it hasn't come back?' she whispered, reaching for Kate's hand and clinging to it.

'No! Oh, no, my love, not that.' For one terrible moment, Kate almost felt that might be easier to deal with. What a mess she had made. Tears squeezed between her lashes and she viewed Polly through a film of moisture. 'I hope you won't hate me when you find out what I've done.'

Something was wrong.

As the ambulance doors closed and Luca stepped back onto the pavement, his attention switched from his patient to Polly. She'd been quieter than normal since the beach picnic, but otherwise fine. They had both enjoyed the hour they had spent on Wednesday visiting Dragan and Melinda and seeing the puppies, and yesterday Polly had spent her afternoon off with Kate. Today, Friday, he had seen her briefly in the staff-room first thing and, while she'd seemed distracted and edgy, there had been nothing to unduly concern him. Given that his own mind had been grappling with the fact that this was the last day he would spend working so closely with Polly, it was possible that he'd not been as observant as usual.

They had joined up during the afternoon to cover the list of home visits—the final ones they would share together as, from next week, he would be assigned a list of his own. Polly had definitely been acting strangely, but he hadn't been able to put his finger on anything specific. However, they had just seen their last patient and were about to head back to the surgery to sign off and go home when an emergency call had come in, diverting them to a woman with chest pain who needed immediate attention.

By the time they'd arrived at the house in The Towans—a hillside road beneath Penhally Heights, the new housing estate that was nearing completion, and a part of the village he'd not been to before—Polly had turned deathly pale. She'd been restless and unfocused, and had looked like someone on the ragged edge of control. One wrong move and he'd feared she would fall. He intended being there to catch her.

Sheer professionalism had allowed him to temporarily switch off his concerns about Polly while he had taken charge of the situation inside the rundown house and attended to the sixty-five-year-old lady who had, undoubtedly, had a heart attack. He had done all he could to keep her stable and comfortable and, although he had wanted nothing more than to find out what was wrong with Polly, he hadn't been able to abandon his patient or risk her taking a turn for the worse before the paramedics arrived.

Now, as the ambulance carrying Mrs Gunn to St Piran pulled away from the kerb, her distressed daughter and son-

in-law following to the hospital by car, Luca was finally free
to focus on Polly. She was already occupying the passenger
seat, he discovered as he stowed his bag in the back, every
atom of her being crying out her tension and inner turmoil.

'Are you OK?' Sliding behind the steering-wheel, he
closed the door, cursing himself for the stupid question. She
was anything *but* OK.

'I'm fine.'

Her smile was over-bright, while her eyes, which had been
strangely blank when they had been in the house a short while
ago, now carried a kind of wildness that made her look like a
cornered animal. One knee was jinking up and down as her foot
tapped repeatedly on the floor, and her hands were clenched
tightly in her lap. As he drove back down The Towans, which
joined Mevagissey Road not far from the church, he glanced
at Polly again, finding her staring straight ahead.

'Would you mind dropping me off in Bridge Street?' she
asked, her voice brittle.

Frowning, Luca nodded. 'Sure.'

A few moments later he was pulling into a parking space
outside Polly's rented flat. Before he had brought the car to
a halt, she was fumbling with the seat belt then the doorhandle, her hands shaking.

'Polly—'

'Sorry to rush. Something I need to do. Thanks, Luca. See
you tomorrow. At the clinic.'

Short, punchy sentences, her voice raw, her breathing too
rapid and uncontrolled. Then she was out of the car, pulling
her bag awkwardly behind her. Switching off the engine, Luca
watched as Polly hurried up the outside stairs that led to the
flat's front door. She stumbled a time or two, struggled with
the lock, then pushed her way inside, leaving the door wide
open. Shaking his head, Luca phoned the surgery, reporting

the status of the patient to Sue, the head receptionist, before having a quick word with Oliver to inform of the situation.

'Go,' his friend told him without delay. 'I'll take care of anything here.'

'Thank you, *mio amico*.'

Free to act, Luca set off in pursuit of Polly. If she thought for one second that he was going to drive away and leave her, she was very much mistaken.

At the top of the wrought-iron stairs, he moved Polly's bag further inside the flat, closed the door and locked it. Then he followed the sounds of panicked breathing and harsh crying, desperately needing to ease her pain and discover its cause. He found her in the bathroom, kneeling on the floor, one hand gripping the basin. His throat tight with emotion, Luca dropped to his knees behind her and wrapped her in his arms. She felt ridiculously fragile and tiny, and he was scared of hugging her too tightly. After a momentary struggle, the fight went out of her, allowing him to hold her close as he absorbed each shudder of her body, every agonised sob tearing holes in his heart.

'Shh. Easy, *mio amore*. You're safe. I'm here, and I'm not going to let anything happen to you.' Hoping to stop her hyperventilating, he whispered soothing words against her ear, one hand moving to stroke the silken strands of hair that fell in an ash-blonde cloud around her shoulders. 'Breathe with me. Slowly, *zingarella*. One at a time. That's it. And again.'

Gradually, Polly's breathing began to quieten and her tears to slow. As she rested limply against him, he reached around her with one hand and moistened the flannel on the side of the basin with cool water. Shifting position, he rose to his feet, scooping Polly up in his arms and carrying her to the small living room. She was as light as a feather, Luca fretted. He sat on the sofa, cradling her on his lap, brushing back her hair so he could gently bathe her face with the flannel.

A ragged sigh escaped her and she let her head rest on his shoulder. Luca closed his eyes for a moment and breathed in the subtle lilac scent of her, relishing the opportunity to hold her close even while hating the reason that had brought it about. Questions fired through his mind but remained unasked…for now.

'I'm sorry,' Polly whispered, the warmth of her breath a soft caress against his neck, her voice raw and rough.

'There is nothing to apologise for.'

Luca eased her up, his heart stuttering as he looked into bruised blue eyes filled with pain, confusion and a definite hint of embarrassment. He wanted to do anything to take those away and to see her happy again. Cupping her face, savouring the downy softness of her skin and tracing the line of her neat, straight nose, the curve of her chin and the shape of her mouth with the pads of his thumbs. He leaned in and pressed kisses to her forehead, the tip of her nose, and an all-too-brief and chaste one to her lips, feeling the shiver of response ripple through her.

'Luca…' She broke off and cleared her throat.

'Would you like some water?'

When she nodded, he eased her off his lap and onto the sofa. He missed the contact, but he'd had to stop before he'd succumbed to temptation. When he kissed her properly, he wanted them both to be consciously aware and involved, not using it as an anaesthetic to mask other emotional events.

In the kitchen, he ran the cold tap and, searching for a glass, discovered the sorry state of her cupboards. A peep in the fridge confirmed that aside from some tired fruit and the remains of the ingredients left over from her baking for the picnic, she had virtually no food in the place. His mind made up, he carried the glass back and handed it to her, waiting while she drank.

'Can you stand?' he asked, supporting her as she rose unsteadily to her feet, not giving her time to argue. 'I'll help you pack what you need.'

She looked adorably befuddled as she stared at him. 'What I'll need for what?'

'You're coming home with me.' Sapphire-blue eyes widened in surprise and alarm. Knowing he didn't have much time, that he had to act before she regained her equilibrium, he stated his case. 'I'm not leaving you alone like this, Polly. Apart from anything else, you have nothing here to eat.'

'I'd planned a take-away after work and shopping at the farmers' market in the morning before the clinic,' she riposted, a flicker of her usual spirit returning.

He believed her—although he suspected she had an issue with food—but he wasn't backing down. 'Either you walk or I carry you. The choice is yours, *zingarella*.'

CHAPTER SEVEN

A FEW hours later Polly still felt shaky. And in shock. Not only because of the emotional turmoil of the last twenty-four hours that had brought her to breaking point but because of how wonderful Luca had been and the way she—who, thanks to Reg and her ex-husband, hated relinquishing control to anyone—had allowed him to take over without so much as a token protest.

Maybe somewhere deep in her subconscious she had known all the time that Luca would come after her. When the storm had hit, cutting her free from her moorings and plunging her into the very depths, it had been Luca who had rescued her, Luca who had held her safe in his arms, Luca who had refused to abandon her.

After leaving the Bridge Street flat, they had collected the twins from Carol. Polly's heart had nearly broken all over again at the way the two little girls had shown such caring concern when their father had explained her presence and told them she wasn't feeling well.

Luca's house was a mile further along the road from where Oliver and Chloe lived in Gatehouse Cottage and Gabriel and Lauren lived in the manor house. In the past they had all belonged to a big estate which had long since been broken up.

Set back from the quiet country road and surrounded by woods and farmland, Polly remembered how rundown Keeper's Cottage had been the last time she'd seen it. Now, the two-storey whitewashed cottage with its slate roof and two squat chimneys had been lovingly renovated. Scarily, she had felt immediately at home.

While Rosie and Toni had watched a DVD and then eaten the supper their father had cooked, Polly had gratefully accepted Luca's suggestion and had indulged in a long, leisurely soak in a hot, fragrant bath. She had emerged, dressed in unflattering but cosy pyjamas, in time to say goodnight to the girls who claimed a hug and a kiss.

'Your phone rang,' Luca told her, gesturing to her mobile that lay on the kitchen table where she had left it. 'I saw Kate's name come up on the display and thought she might worry if you didn't answer. I just said that you were here and would phone back when you were free. I hope that's OK.'

'Thanks, Luca.' The small gesture was kind and thoughtful to both Kate and herself...but a flush had warmed her cheeks as she wondered what Kate thought and if she was adding two plus two and making ten.

'There's plenty of Bolognese, Polly, and we have some blackcurrant cheesecake in the fridge,' Luca had added, ushering his charges towards the stairs. 'Help yourself to them, or anything else you want, while I get these two bathed and then to bed.' He paused and met her gaze. 'Then we'll talk.'

So thankful was she for the opportunity to eat alone—especially with the irresistible temptation of dessert—that Polly gave Kate a quick call and was halfway through her helping of the delicious spaghetti dish Luca had made before his final words sank in and brought her down to earth with a bump. It was unsurprising that he had questions...and wanted answers. But how much should she tell him? There were things even Kate didn't know, Polly acknowledged, especially about Charles. Things she hoped never to reveal. So why was there a desire—almost a compulsion—to tell Luca?

Although she had been fighting hard since the first moment she had set eyes on him, every day spent with Luca had further weakened her resolve. She had known him barely two weeks and already it mattered far too much what he thought of her. How would he react if he knew the truth? The mistakes she had made and the things she had done—as a teenager and, later, in her marriage—would no doubt shock and appall him. The thought of him disgusted and disappointed in her was too horrible to contemplate.

Restless, Polly cleared the table and washed up, but her brain continued on the same track. What was it about Luca that caused her to act so out of character? The strength of the connection between them and the potency of her attraction to him were beyond her experience—and she found it impossible to believe that such a sexy and supremely masculine man like Luca could ever be interested in a someone like her... Plain Polly from Penhally.

Her troubled thoughts fragmented when she heard Luca's footsteps descending the stairs, and her tension increased. She was running out of time...and diversions.

'Hi,' he greeted her, the husky timbre of his voice sending tingles down her spine. 'Everything all right?'

Polly nodded. It was the only response she could manage as she had forgotten how to breathe when Luca walked into the kitchen and bestowed on her one of the special smiles that turned her bones to jelly. He'd changed out of the suit he had worn to work. Now jeans encased long, athletically muscled legs, the denim so worn and faded that it clung lovingly to him like a second skin. And his feet were bare. For some reason that was shockingly intimate and arousing.

A black cashmere sweater shaped his impressive torso, the hem riding up to reveal a tantalising glimpse of olive-toned flesh when he stretched his arms above his head and yawned. The sleeves were pushed up to his elbows, exposing strong, hair-brushed forearms…arms that had held her with such care and tenderness.

'The Bolognese was lovely.'

'You had some?' His genuine pleasure and the warm intimacy of his smile made her tingle all over. 'I'm glad. Is there anything else I can get you?'

'No, thanks. I hope you don't mind, but…' Polly paused, hating it that she was still so afflicted by the conditioning of her childhood.

As Luca gave her his full attention and slowly closed the gap between them, Polly's heart fluttered. 'Mind what, *zingarella*?'

'I, um…' Again her words trailed off and she fought the inbuilt programming that encouraged her to deny what she most enjoyed. 'I did take some cheesecake.'

'Of course I don't mind. I told you to help yourself to anything you wanted.' Her skin tingled and she sucked in a shaky breath as his hands cupped her face. 'Why do you feel it is wrong if you enjoy something?'

Polly shook her head. The question hit right at the heart of one of the main issues she was trying so hard to understand and reconcile. One of those ghosts Kate said she had to face if she was ever to move on. She looked into dark, dark eyes, warmth stealing across her cheeks as he studied her intently. His perception and instinctive reading of her were scary. She was aware the instant his expression changed. The blood turned thick and hot in her veins as Luca grazed one thumb across the sensitive skin at the corner of her mouth.

'You have some blackcurrant here.'

'O-oh…'

The pad of his thumb pressed against her mouth, silencing her mumbled reply. Her lips parted instinctively to the gentle pressure and his voice dropped to a throaty purr as he issued his instruction. 'Lick.'

Polly told herself to resist the temptation to obey, but her body had a will of its own. Her disobedient tongue peeped out, shy at first and then bolder as his thumb slipped between her lips to meet it and the tangy masculine taste of him exploded in her mouth. Luca slowly moved his moistened thumb and wiped at the fruit stain he had found. Without breaking eye contact he raised the thumb to his own mouth, his eyes half closing as he sucked on it, as if savouring *her*.

It was a simple gesture but so incredibly erotic that an involuntary whimper escaped as Polly watched him. Every part of her was on fire, and an aching knot of need tightened deep inside her, driving her crazy. One tiny taste of his skin had left her craving more. His touch, his closeness, his subtle earthy aroma…everything about him robbed her of common sense.

'Luca—'

Polly heard the hitch in her voice. Everything was so jumbled up inside her, her emotions raw and near the surface, especially after the last twenty-four hours, and having Luca witness her loss of control. And now, as if she hadn't enough to resolve, her feelings for Luca were confusing her.

Before she'd had a chance to regain her equilibrium, Luca held out a hand, waiting patiently for her acquiescence. While part of her mind questioned the way she had so meekly allowed him to take charge, she found herself sliding her hand into his, feeling at once enveloped by his strength. Switching out the kitchen light, Luca led her to the cosy living room which had a surprisingly high beamed ceiling, pastel-painted walls and a Cornish bluestone floor covered with rugs. A welcoming fire burned in the stone and slate fireplace. Luca added a couple more logs, dimmed the lights and then, before she could draw breath or raise a protest, Polly found herself lifted off her feet and cradled in his arms once more.

Choosing a comfortable armchair, he sat down with her on his lap. One arm supported her back, the palm of his hand cupped possessively over her hip, while his other arm draped across her legs, his hand resting on her leg, just above her knee. She was acutely aware of every point of contact—acutely aware of *him*. For a few moments the only sounds penetrating the silence were the crackling of the fire. Tense and uncertain, Polly stared into the flickering flames.

'I hope you know that neither Kate nor I would betray any confidences,' Luca said, reclaiming her attention, the sincerity in his voice undeniable.

'I know.' And she did. Even if she was confused about everything else. 'What did she say when she rang earlier?'

'That the two of you had an emotional time together yesterday.' The hand at her knee stroked up and down her thigh, soothing yet arousing. 'Does that have anything to do with what happened this afternoon?'

Polly tried to refocus her scattered thoughts. 'Indirectly.' What she couldn't tell him about was the big secret Kate had confided to her.

She was still in shock after those revelations. And exhausted from the tears both she and Kate had shed as they had hugged each other. First had come the stunning confession that *Nick Tremayne* was Jem's real father, followed by the circumstances that had brought it about on the fateful night of the big storm eleven years ago. How had Kate coped, carrying that burden for so long? Yet she had raised Jem alone, and lived with the grief and guilt. How Polly wished she had known and could have done something to help all those years. And how could Kate have thought for one moment that she, Polly, would judge her or hate her? Never! More tears had flowed.

Kate had explained the awful circumstances that had led to Nick learning the truth about his son fifteen months ago—and how badly he had behaved to Kate and Jem since. Polly still felt emotionally raw and shocked, but she couldn't share any of that with Luca because she had promised to keep Kate's confidence. Only a handful of people besides Kate and Nick knew the truth…and now she did too.

On top of learning Kate's secret, there had been the talk of the beach picnic, Polly's eating issues and her reaction to Luca and his daughters. With mention of her own past, her return to Penhally and the ghosts she still had to face, it had been an emotional roller-coaster—and that had been without laying open the wreckage of her marriage or touching on the no-go area of her lost daughter. In view of all that, it was hardly surprising that last call to The Towans had been a shock too far.

'Talk to me, *zingarella*.' Luca's softly voiced words brought her crashing back to reality. 'You'd been on edge all day, but it was when that last call came in that you zoned out on me. I suspect sheer force of will made you hang on until we reached the flat. If it was nothing to do with your visit to Kate yesterday, what was it?'

How much could she tell Luca? It was scary to even consider opening herself up to inevitable pain reliving old memories would cause, and to making herself so vulnerable to another person. But maybe Kate was right—however difficult, maybe it was time to face some of her demons. Perversely, Luca was both the first and last person in whom she wanted to confide. The first because even in such a short time she had come to trust him, and although she had tried to keep herself apart, the deep connection between them was impossible to deny. And the last because exposing dark secrets and opening herself ran the risk of him thinking less of her.

Releasing a shaky breath, she leaned against him, resting her head on his shoulder, her face so close to his neck she could breath in his musky male scent and feel the warmth of his smooth, olive-toned skin.

'I don't know where to start,' she finally whispered, resolved to divulge at least some of her past. 'Or what you'll think.'

Polly's softly spoken words brought a lump to Luca's throat.

'Do you trust me?' he asked, relieved that her nod of assent came with no hesitation. It humbled him. 'Thank you.'

Polly raised her head and looked at him, puzzlement evident. 'What for?'

'I don't think you trust easily, or often, so I'm honoured…' He lifted his hand from her thigh, his fingers stroking the softness of one pale cheek. 'I won't let you down.'

'You'll probably wish you'd never met me.'

Her attempt at light-heartedness fell flat, her words revealing a genuine fear, one he was determined to set to rest. 'Look at me, *zingarella*.' Slowly, reluctantly, her lashes opened to reveal bruised blue eyes. Luca cupped her chin, holding her gaze, praying she would recognise his sincerity. 'I care about you, I respect you, and I admire you. You can talk to me about anything, at any time, and nothing you say will change how I feel. Nothing. OK?' he finished, feeling emotional himself as Polly nodded again and he saw the unshed tears she was battling to contain.

Luca breathed a sigh of relief at the small gesture of Polly's trust in him. Everything he had learned about her these past two weeks had shown him it was not something she granted lightly. It was a small breakthrough, and he welcomed it, but knew it was only one step on what might be a long journey.

Thank God for Kate. He thought back to the moment earlier in the evening when he had answered Polly's mobile phone. He had explained what had happened without giving more away than necessary, relieved when Kate had given him her wholehearted support.

Without breaking any confidences, the older woman had managed to impart some useful tips. One of which had been her advice not to make an issue of food, and to leave the room if he wanted Polly to eat anything. It had sounded strange, but he had followed Kate's guidance, and it had worked. Just to make sure, he had peeped round the kitchen door to see her tucking into a plate of spaghetti Bolognese with relish. He had been relieved she was eating, grateful to Kate for the guidance and even more intrigued about her relationship with food.

'Can you tell me now?' he asked, eager for her to begin talking. 'What happened today? What was it about that last call that brought things to a head?'

Luca felt a shudder run through Polly's slight frame. 'I— um… The house…' Again she broke off, one hand fluttering nervously. He caught it, linking their fingers, trying to convey his support.

'The house,' he encouraged.

'Yes.' Her eyes closed briefly and when they opened again, they were so full of pain that the breath locked in his chest. 'It was the house I lived in for the first seventeen and a half years of my life. I'd not been there since I left Penhally and being called out there was so unexpected. Having to walk through that front door again brought everything crashing down around me. It was even more of a shock because although there was a long delay in selling it after Reg died four years ago, I assumed the new owner would have improved and redecorated it by now. That it wouldn't mean anything to me. Seeing it, cleaner but otherwise much as it was when I lived there, really hit me and threw me back to the horror of that time.'

As an involuntary shudder rippled through Polly, her fingers tightened painfully on his, but Luca didn't care. Any short-lived discomfort was as nothing compared to that which Polly had so clearly endured. No wonder she had reacted so strongly, being confronted with her past that way. He had so many questions but he forced himself to silence, waiting for Polly to take this at her own pace, feeling the tension in her fragile frame.

'Kate told me that Reg Searle was a handsome man when he was young, a charmer, a master of manipulation and used to getting whatever he wanted,' she began, her voice shaky and uncertain. 'And he wanted my mother. She was just out of school, quiet and shy, clever and beautiful, and she fell for Reg, five years older, in an instant. She became pregnant with me very quickly, married Reg and gave up every dream she ever had for herself and her career as a teacher.'

'*Scusami*…I am sorry,' he murmured, raising their joined hands and brushing his lips over the inside of her wrist, feeling the steady, over-fast beat of her pulse.

Polly bit her lip, her eyes closing momentarily before she opened them again. 'Reg very quickly became bitter and resentful.' She turned her head to stare at the fire.

Luca followed her gaze, wondering what she saw in the flickering flames. He noticed how she never referred to the man as her father. A tight knot formed inside him—anxiety at all the things he had yet to learn about the man and his effect on Polly's development.

'Reg expected everything to be handed to him on a plate, blaming his failings on everyone else, chasing one hopeless get-rich-quick scheme after another and hating to see others succeed. That other people worked hard for what they had didn't seem to register with him,' she continued after a moment, shaking her head. 'He needed to control everything and everyone, most especially my mother, blaming her for his downfall, for holding him back. More and more he turned to drink and to gambling. He wasn't physically violent, but he was verbally and emotionally cruel. Quite early on he lost everything, including his looks and his charm, and he became an embittered, lazy, unpleasant man. And when my mother died, he turned all that frustration and resentment on me.'

'Polly…' Her name whispered out on an agonised breath as a painful image formed in Luca's mind of a fragile child—hardly older than his own girls were now—left in the charge of a bullying man who had no right to call himself a father.

'The first sign of what was to come was when he took Barney away.' Her explanation rushed on, as if she would never start again if she stopped. 'At four, I didn't understand. All I recognised was his perverse pleasure in making other people miserable. Me especially. I soon learned that anything I enjoyed or took pleasure in was taken away or spoiled or forbidden. Over the years, any academic or other achievement was punished, because having someone, especially a child, do well or be successful, served only to highlight his own failures.'

Luca turned his head, nuzzling the graceful curve on her neck, breathing in her scent, wishing he could have been there to make a difference to Polly's life. 'What happened?' Somehow Luca forced the words out, not at all sure he could bear to learn more of Polly's unhappy background, but knowing he needed to, for her sake as much as his own. He couldn't change her past—but he hoped to find a way to make her future a happy one.

'With Reg it was verbal abuse and control. When it goes on for so long and is so insidious, it wears you down and you believe it. He belittled me constantly, about everything, from being stupid to the way I looked…' As she paused, Luca worried what slight she was remembering. 'It was all about him having control over me. I don't like to admit it, but I learned to be sneaky and to lie, to deceive him. If I hid the things I liked most, like books and animals and learning, they weren't taken away from me. And if I pretended to like the things I really hated, I could avoid them.'

'Self-preservation. You were one smart cookie even then,' he praised, rewarded when she turned her head and met his gaze, a tiny smile curving her mouth. A mouth he could not help but drop a swift kiss upon.

A hint of pink washed her cheeks and she ducked her head, relaxing more in his arms, her fingers still linked with his. 'There were constant putdowns about how I looked and acted and behaved. I never had friends. Or things—money was so tight and whatever he had went on his drink and gambling. The house was filthy and falling into disrepair, much to the annoyance of the neighbours. I think I knew, even quite young, that education was my way out. If only I could hang on until I left school.' A humorous laugh escaped. 'I must have been the only child with a parent who was angry if I got good grades and a favourable report. That's where Kate and my headmistress, Ms Stanbury, really triumphed,' she added, a genuine smile acting like a sudden sunny break in the clouds.

'What did they do?' Luca asked, intrigued.

'I confided in them about the reports and grades, and from then on, until I finished school, Ms Stanbury kept my real reports locked away in the safe for me to take when I left, and made sure that a false report, one with poor grades and worrying about my lack of ambition and success, was sent to Reg.'

Luca wanted to hug Ms Stanbury for the stroke of ingenuity—one which could have landed her in trouble had she been found out. 'Did it work?'

'Like a charm. He would open the report and—' She broke off, a shiver running through her, and Luca tightened his hold.

'And?' he prompted as she settled again.

She ran her free hand over her face as if trying to scrub away an image or a memory. 'I can see the sly, mocking smile now as he told me how thick and stupid I was, that I'd never amount to anything, just like my mother. There were times I longed to tell him the joke was on him, but I never did. Somehow I always managed to hold onto the bigger picture…counting down the days until I could get away.'

'How did you survive it, *zingarella*?' he asked, haunted by the thought of what she had been through.

'By turning into a person I didn't like…a bad person.'

Luca shook his head. 'You are not a bad person,' he insisted, stroking her hair as she turned her face into his shoulder.

'I hated him,' she admitted, her voice rising. 'For years all I had inside me was hate and anger. I wished *he* was dead and not my mother. Everyone loathed him, and me by association. He never lost an opportunity to belittle me in front of other people and I hid from everyone, trying not to be noticed.' She paused, drawing in an angry breath. 'I looked for ways to get back at him, but he took everything from me that mattered, Luca.' A sob escaped and his throat tightened at her distress, making it hard to breathe.

'Those photograph albums Kate mentioned—they were the only pictures I had of my mother, including a few of me with her. I stashed them away, tried to protect them until I could sneak them out to Kate. But Reg found them. He said I was a thief, that the pictures weren't mine and that I had to be punished. I was seven.' Tears spilled down her cheeks, and Luca's heart broke for her. 'He took me outside, holding me by my hair as I fought him, laughing as he burned all the pictures and made me watch. I tried so hard to hold onto her but I can't remember her face clearly now.'

Luca wrapped his arms around her, feeling guilty that he had pushed her to talk and opened up all this pain. 'That's not your fault, *zingarella*. It's one of the painful effects of loss. I make sure the children have pictures and memories of their mother, but after nearly four years, the images in my mind are becoming fuzzier around the edges, and more and more I need the pictures to help me remember,' he told her, and she raised her head, understanding and empathy in tear-stained eyes.

'It hurts,' she whispered.

'I know, *mio amore*. I know.' Facing his own pain, he laid more of himself bare in the hope of giving her comfort. 'I didn't have the problems you did growing up, but my parents were archaeologists. They were both Italian, but they met when studying at university in Cambridge. Their work meant they spent weeks, months at a time out in the field, and when I came along—unplanned—I was a hindrance, in the way around digs, so as I grew older, I was left behind. At first I stayed with my only surviving grandparent, my mother's mother, but after she died when I was eleven, I was sent to boarding school in England. I always felt different. Apart. That I had only myself. Which was the case when my parents were killed in an accident in South America when I was sixteen. I saw them so rarely, I hardly remember them.'

'Oh, Luca…'

He shook his head, moved at her capacity for caring and kindness, even at the height of her own distress. 'My situation was nothing like yours. I shared it only to try and show I understood the emotions and the importance of photographs and memories. I just wish there had been someone who could have helped you. Why did no one intervene?' he demanded hoarsely, feeling continuing rage that Polly had been treated so badly.

'Kate tried, but Reg made life difficult for her and her husband James, and kept them from seeing me. As I got older, I'd find ways to meet Kate without Reg knowing, but it was risky,' she told him, her voice thick with emotion. 'Ms Stanbury tried, too. But although he was mean and had a nasty temper, Reg was sharp enough never to do anything physical to hurt me that would have allowed the authorities to step in. Even when I was ill…'

'You were ill?' Anxiety gripped him as her words trailed off. 'What happened?'

She exhaled a ragged breath, and Luca kept her close. 'From the age of eleven to seventeen I had…' Again she hesitated, and Luca held his breath, waiting for her to continue. Lashes lowered, hiding myriad emotions, while her fingers clung ever more resolutely to his. 'I was anorexic,' she finally whispered, hiding her face against him.

Luca took a moment, wrestling with an array of thoughts or feelings, one of which was a strange kind of relief because so much was now explained. But he needed to know more. Equally important was the need to show Polly his support. He eased her head up, his heart squeezing at the embarrassment and shame shadowed in her eyes, emotions he desperately wanted to erase.

Cupping her chin, he leaned in and pressed a soft, lingering kiss to her lips, drawing back as he felt the answering response within her. 'You felt food, and what went into your body, was the only thing you could control?' he asked softly, seeing her eyes widen in surprise at his understanding.

'Yes. That was one aspect of it.'

'Tell me,' he invited, adjusting their positions so she was resting comfortably against him, feeling the sigh that shuddered through her.

'It was a combination of things. Control, as you said. Also punishment…for Reg. And self-punishment for me.'

Luca frowned. 'Why for you? Nothing was your fault.'

'You live like that for so long and things become twisted,' she explained. 'The harsher and more verbally abusive Reg became, the stricter my eating regimes. He ran me down so much that I felt worthless, and during my early teens his taunts just echoed in my head, even when he wasn't around. I had no friends. I tried to shrink myself, to hide. I was the skinny kid who kept in the background, never speaking, always with her nose in a book. And Reg's words went round and round that I didn't deserve anything.'

'Polly—'

'It was drummed into me from the age of four that I didn't deserve nice things, that I couldn't have what I wanted or enjoyed, and I somehow turned that round in my own mind to use food as a control,' she told him, shaking her head, the fingers of her free hand picking at the hem of her pyjama top.

Luca didn't know what to say. He was scared at what could have happened to her, filled with admiration for all she had overcome, and utterly determined that she should have everything she wanted—all the good things she deserved—to make her happy for the rest of her life.

'You're an amazing and inspirational young woman, Polly Carrick.'

Luca's husky words, and the sincere admiration and warmth in his eyes, took Polly's breath away. She shook her head. How could he say that after what she had told him? 'No, I—' Her protest was silenced as two fingertips pressed against her lips.

'To have overcome your childhood with such a brutish man is extraordinary enough, but to add in five or six years battling against anorexia while still keeping up your educa-

tion is incredible, *zingarella*,' he insisted, her skin awash with
sensation as his fingers trailed across her cheek and down her
neck, making it hard for her to concentrate. 'You have shown
such strength of character to face and overcome all you have.
You should be proud of yourself.' Smiling, he brushed another
soft and tantalising kiss on her mouth. '*I'm* proud of you.'

Polly didn't know what to say. It had been harrowing,
dredging up so much from her past, things she had tried to
suppress for so long because they hurt so much, but which her
return to Penhally and especially revisiting the house she had
lived in had brought back to the surface. Facing old demons
was tough, but Luca had been the amazing one, offering her
support and understanding.

'And now?' he queried, still keeping her as close as was
possible in the confines of the chair. 'Do you still have issues
with food? Do you still deny yourself the things you like?'

'Not exactly.'

A heart-stopping smile brought the dimple to one lean
cheek. 'How exactly?'

'I'm mostly OK with food now.' She hesitated, her gaze
sliding from his. She wished she could lie, but he was scarily
insightful. He was also non-judgemental and that gave her the
confidence to carry on. 'I find it difficult eating in public or
in front of people. There's still a tiny part of me that feels I
have to deny myself things I most want, that I can't be extrava-
gant or enjoy anything but the basics.'

'Thank you, again, for trusting me.'

'Thank you for listening,' she whispered back.

She didn't know who moved first, but the small gap
between them narrowed and her lips met his in another slow,
lingering, gentle kiss. Red-hot passion and urgent need shim-
mered around the edges, but as if they both shared a silent
agreement, it didn't get out of hand. Yet. For Polly it was

almost more erotic and sensual. It was also important, like the silent sealing of some kind of vow.

'It's late,' Luca murmured when they finally broke apart, one hand stroking the wavy strands of her hair. 'I think you've had enough for one day. If I make us some hot chocolate, will you drink it?'

'Yes.'

Her agreement earned her another special smile. As she slid off his lap, she immediately missed the closeness. She went to use the bathroom, her mind in a whirl as she thought back over the evening and how wonderful Luca had been, how easy to talk to. It had been hard and emotional to face many of the issues, but she was surprised to find she felt much better for having confided in him. Some barrier had been crossed tonight. She knew it, was scared by it, and yet there was no urge to run away from it.

Unable to resist, she peeped in the doorway of the twins' bedroom. She had been given a tour of the room earlier by the girls who were proud of their space, especially the feature wall that depicted a forest scene with lots of exotic animals. Polly had been amazed to discover Luca had painted it for them, revealing a talent she hadn't known he possessed.

Now the room was in darkness, save for the nightlight on the chest between the twin beds. Near it, Polly knew, was a photo cube that contained several photos of Elaine. She had experienced mixed emotions looking at the images, seeing for the first time the woman Luca had loved and lost, who'd been so much the opposite of herself. Elaine, she'd discovered, had been tall and athletic and curvy, with auburn hair, green eyes and a wide, vibrant smile. Polly had felt dowdy and inadequate and unfeminine in comparison. And despairing. How could Luca possibly be interested in her, having been married to such a woman?

Sighing, she looked down at the shadowed shapes of the

twins. Toni was sprawled on her front, one small hand clasped round the leg of a soft, plush grey elephant who sat protectively on the pillow. Smiling, Polly straightened the duvet. Her gaze switched to Rosie who was on one side and curled in a foetal position, one arm wrapped around her favourite companion, a cuddly Winnie the Pooh. Neither of the girls stirred. For a moment Polly listened to the sound of their breathing, her heart squeezing with emotion. She was alarmed how much they and their father had taken over her life in two short weeks.

Exhaustion overtook her as she left the girls and walked along to the far end of the upstairs corridor to Luca's bedroom. The spare room had yet to be furnished, he had told her earlier, and they had already had one debate about using the sofa, which she had lost. She sat on the edge of the huge bed and knew she didn't want to be there alone. But…

Luca's arrival forestalled her thoughts. 'Thanks.' She accepted the mug and sipped her drink, watching as he went to a chest of drawers and pulled out a T-shirt and pair of boxers. Setting down his own mug, he disappeared into the en suite. The low ache deep inside her begun to tighten, and her hands gripped her mug as she listened to the sounds of him undressing. When he returned to the main room, she kept her head down, anxious not to be caught staring at him.

'What's wrong?'

His voice broke the growing tension that had descended. She shook her head, unable to ask.

'Polly?' He hunkered down in front of her, taking her empty mug and setting it aside before cupping her chin and tilting up her face. 'Talk to me.'

She stared into deep brown eyes and feared he now owned he soul. 'I don't want to be alone, but…'

'But you're not yet ready for anything else to happen between us,' he finished for her with gentle understanding, his fingers stroking her cheek. 'Do not worry, *mio amore*, I had no intention of leaving you. Now, into bed with you.'

As he moved and turned back the duvet for her, she slid underneath, trying to mask her nervousness with a light-hearted comment. 'You must be used to putting little girls to bed!'

His chuckle resonated to every nerve-ending. 'I can assure you, Polly, that you are not a little girl in my eyes, and I do not feel remotely fatherly towards you,' he added, the sexy rumble of his voice causing the breath to stutter in her lungs. 'I want to make love with you,' he continued huskily, sliding into bed and making her pulse race as he snuggled up behind her and wrapped her in his arms, drawing her back into him. 'I hope it will happen when we are both ready. But there is no pressure, *zingarella*.' He was silent for a moment, but then his next words, so softly spoken, shocked her. 'I have not even looked at another woman since Elaine, let alone held or kissed or slept with one. I've waited nearly four years. I can wait a bit longer, OK?'

'OK.' Tears stung her eyes as the enormity of what he had said sank in. And he knew, his fingers there to wipe the wetness from her cheeks. 'I'm sorry. I *never* cry. Not usually.'

'These are not usual times, *mio amore*. You are going through a difficult process to lay the past to rest that's never easy. I meant what I said,' he continued, his whole being cocooning her in warmth and safety in the darkness. I am proud of you. And I'll be here with you every step of the way. If you want me to. I know there is more you need to deal with—here in Penhally, and with whatever it is that makes you sad when you look at the girls—and I'm here to listen whenever you are ready.'

Her throat was so thick with emotion that a hoarse 'Thank you' was all she could manage.

'Sleep now, *zingarella*. I will not let anything happen to you.'

Instinctively Polly snuggled deeper into his embrace, breathing in the scent of his musky male aroma, feeling safe, but also on the cusp of something dangerously exciting. She had still not dared to ask what his nickname for her meant, but that he said it in the same affectionate tone as he did the loving endearments for his children made her feel warm and cherished for the first time in her life.

Luca was wonderful and she didn't deserve him. Or his girls. He had taken everything she had thrown at him and he said he was ready for more. In the darkness, she listened to his steady breathing and the regular beat of his heart. Her hands clung to the arm wrapped strong and sure around her waist.

A silent tear squeezed between her lashes and trickled down her cheek.

What would he say—and would he still be there—when he found out that she had killed her baby?

CHAPTER EIGHT

'THANK you, Polly. It takes a while to stir these old bones to action.'

Jane Watson smiled her appreciation as Polly held the Zimmer frame steady and helped the older lady rise stiffly to her feet. Once up, she paused a moment, a faint grimace on her face as she allowed painful joints to adjust and settle.

'Just take your time.'

Glancing through the front window of the ground-floor flat in the sheltered-housing unit, Polly could see Luca chatting to Brian Watson as he ushered the twins out to the car. As always when looking at him, her breath hitched, her pulse raced and myriad conflicting thoughts and emotions filled her mind.

The news that they were to visit to the twins' grandparents on Sunday morning, before going to the riding stables, had terrified Polly. How could she possibly go with Luca and his children to visit his late wife's parents? A second question had followed closely on the heels of the first. Whatever would they think? Of her—and of her inclusion as part of their group?

As it turned out, she had been taken aback by the warmth of the Watsons' welcome and their ready acceptance of her presence. She had been grateful for Luca's silent support and encouragement, and she knew instinctively that he was watching out for her. But it hadn't been necessary. As he had promised her, there had been no awkwardness at all. Elaine was remembered with love and affection but Polly sensed all was being done to move on and make life normal and exciting and full of promise for the children.

Polly had been concerned by the frailness of both Jane and Brian, and understood Luca's relief that the older couple were now living somewhere that allowed them to maintain some independence and yet had help on hand twenty-four hours a day. With Brian's heart condition and Jane's rheumatoid arthritis and asthma, it was a miracle they had kept so active for so long and had managed any care of the twins in the early years. Polly hoped that now the couple were settled in the sheltered-housing flat, they would follow Luca's advice and register with the Penhally Bay Surgery. She would be honoured to be part of the team to care for them.

'Can I do anything for you before we go?' Polly queried now.

'No, my love, but bless you for asking. Oh, it's been so wonderful meeting you!'

Surprised, Polly found herself drawn into an awkward embrace, the Zimmer frame between them. 'Thank you and Brian for making me so welcome. And for sharing with me your memories of my mother,' she added, her voice tinged with emotion.

She had been amazed to discover that Jane had known her mother, had been her teacher at school—a little surprise Luca had dropped on her as they had arrived that morning. To hear anecdotes wholly new to her about Yvonne and Kate as young teenagers had been a special and unexpected gift she would treasure.

'I hope we can now look forward to seeing you often,' the older woman said as she made her way slowly towards the door. 'Brian and I are so grateful to you.'

'To me? But why?' Polly exclaimed in astonishment.

Jane's smile was engaging, almost girlish. 'You have brought happiness and real smiles to the faces of Luca and the girls these last two weeks. Forgive an old woman her interference. Luca hasn't shown interest in anything but the girls or his work. Of course his grief and his mixed emotions over all that happened were natural when Elaine died—it was a shock and a loss for us all.' She paused a moment, sadness evident in her eyes. 'Brian and I have been worried as more time has gone by and Luca has continued to ignore his own happiness. We've spoken of it to him, he knows he has our support when he is ready to move on. But he showed no sign of it. He's a wonderful man and an excellent father.' Her deep affection apparent, Jane's gaze moved to the tableau outside the window.

'Yes, he is,' Polly admitted softly, watching him tease Toni.

Shifting position to make herself more comfortable, Jane turned to face her and Polly couldn't look away from the warmth in the older woman's gaze. 'A lot of female doctors and nurses at St Piran Hospital tried to get themselves noticed, but Luca was blind to them all. Brian and I despaired. Then, two weeks ago, Luca met you.'

'Oh, but… I don't think…' Polly's confused reply came to a halt when Jane smiled and laid a hand on her arm.

'I don't mean to make you uncomfortable, my love. Far from it. I just wanted you to know that Brian and I have no reservations—quite the opposite. You have our blessing.'

Embarrassed and unsure, Polly was saved from answering as the door opened and Luca stepped inside. 'Are you ready to go?' he asked.

'Yes.' Polly met his gaze, noting how his eyes narrowed as he studied her, as if he could read her agitation. 'I was just on my way out.'

He stepped closer, resting a hand at the small of her back. 'Is everything all right?

'Fine,' Polly answered, hoping her smile wasn't as shaky as it felt.

'I think I ran a bit ahead of myself,' Jane admitted, her tone apologetic. 'I was trying to reassure Polly that Brian and I are wholly in favour and supportive of you both.'

Luca gave her a gentle squeeze, keeping her close. 'Thank you, Jane. I'm sorry to rush, but I arranged to meet Georgina at the riding stables at eleven,' he explained, acknowledging his mother-in-law's sentiments but neatly changing the subject, Polly noticed.

'Of course, you must go. The girls are so excited!' Jane laughed, giving Luca a kiss and hug. 'I shall look forward to hearing all about it.' Smiling, she turned her frame to a better angle and Polly found herself hugged again, then Jane rested the palm of one frail, papery hand against her cheek and shook her head. 'You look so like your mother, it's uncanny.'

'Really? Oh, no, I don't think so. Although maybe we had similar hair colour,' Polly murmured in protest, unable to believe it. The features of her mother's face had long been hazy, but she knew Yvonne had been beautiful—just as she knew that she, Plain Polly from Penhally, was not.

Polly's mind was buzzing as they said their final goodbyes to Jane and Brian. She would have thought she had dreamed the last couple of days if they hadn't been so real. Two nights running she had lain in Luca's arms in his bed. As well as sleeping better than ever before in her life, she also felt jumpy and on edge...and finding it increasingly difficult to resist the temptation to either ravish Luca or beg him to ravish her—or both.

She had woken on Saturday morning to find herself alone in bed, but the girls had come running, clambering over her and bestowing hugs and kisses as they gave her a thirty-minute call for breakfast. They had all visited the farmers' market together, and then Rosie and Toni had gone happily to the childminder, while Luca had accompanied her to the surgery for the clinic. It had been a busy but rewarding session, and she had been grateful for Luca's help and admiring of his skill.

Nothing had been discussed or decided, but instead of returning to the flat as Polly had expected to—and, indeed, had told herself she must—Saturday night had found her back at Keeper's Cottage. The girls had been adorable. They seemed to find nothing peculiar about her presence in their house— or their father's bed. Luca didn't make a big issue of it but remained open and truthful with them.

Polly had worried in case the girls mentioned it to anyone at school, or to their grandparents, concerned for any effect it might have on Luca more than herself, but he wasn't bothered at all.

'We have done nothing wrong, *zingarella*. It is no one else's business.'

Luca had spoken the words more than once over the weekend and Polly knew they were true. They hadn't done anything wrong. They hadn't done anything at all—yet. A shiver of fearful anticipation rippled thorough her. She knew Luca was giving her time to feel comfortable, to be ready—knew, too, that it had been as long for him as it had for her since being intimate with anyone—but all that succeeded in doing was to ratchet up the tension and cause simmering expectation. Some time soon, the cauldron was going to boil over and that both scared and excited her. As much because she knew there were things she had not yet told him. And, when it happened, it meant facing another inner fear. Having Luca see the body she hated.

For now she was taking each moment as it came and marvelling how, in such a short time, she had become immersed in the d'Azzaro family's lives. Things had changed so dramatically in a matter of hours, without her conscious thought or choosing, and it was almost as if she was living someone else's life. A fantasy life that surely had to end, crashing her back to earth and reality with a bump.

A light touch on her arm pulled her sharply from her reverie and she turned to look at Luca. 'Hmm...did I miss something?' she murmured, warmth stealing through her in response to the slow-burn smile he sent her.

'Which way, *zingarella*?'

'Oh.' She sat up straighter in her seat and looked around to see where they were, amazed to discover they had almost reached their destination. 'Goodness, we've arrived in no time at all,' she told him, thankful there was no other traffic on the road as Luca kept the engine idling and waited patiently at the crossroads. 'It seemed to take for ever to get here in the old days when I had to pedal a rusty old bicycle!' Embarrassed that she had been rambling on, and that the emotions the memories evoked were showing in the shakiness of her voice, she cleared her throat and gave him the information he needed. 'Take a right here, and it's about half a mile down on the left-hand side.'

'Are you all right?' Luca asked, lowering his voice so that the twins, chattering together in the back, could not hear him.

'Fine,' Polly managed, not at all sure that she was.

His fingers lingered a moment longer before he withdrew them and moved his hand to put the car in gear. 'Is this the first time you have come out here since returning to Penhally?'

'Yes. It feels strange,' she admitted after a pause, her voice low.

'If at any time it's too much and you want to go, promise you will tell me.'

Luca's husky demand took her by surprise. Her gaze met his, and she saw the understanding in deep brown eyes. His intuition was scary sometimes. They had met two weeks ago. But he *knew* her. How could he see inside her soul? 'Luca, I—'

'Promise me,' he insisted.

The silent battle of wills didn't last long. Sighing, Polly nodded her head. 'OK.'

As Luca pulled away from the crossroads, Polly wiped suddenly damp palms down the thighs of the loose-fitting jeans she had worn, more appropriate for the occasion than her customary gypsy skirts. A knot formed in her stomach as they approached the entrance to the stables. The sign at the end of the drive was new—bright and informative without being ostentatious—and Georgina's name now had pride of place along with her husband's as owners and instructors.

A hundred yards down the unpaved track brought them to an extended parking area, a gate preventing people from driving to the yard itself. Polly climbed out, breathing in the country air and the familiar scents as they all walked towards the main yard.

'OK, *bambine*. Team talk.' Luca gathered the twins to him and hunkered down, causing the denim jeans to tauten over muscled thighs and taut rear, raising Polly's temperature several degrees. 'Do you remember what we said about the way to behave around animals and in the stables?'

Two dark heads nodded in agreement. Polly's throat tightened as she watched the little tableau in front of her…caring father and devoted daughters at once angelic and mischievous. At the moment, the girls wore identical expressions, managing to combine solemn concentration as they watched their father through big brown eyes with the bubbling excitement at what was to come. She wanted to hug them. And Luca.

'Yes, Papà. We're to talk quietly and we mustn't rush around,' Rosie said, sending her father a sweet smile.

Toni shifted from side to side with pent-up energy. 'And we do what you and Polly and the horse lady tell us to do.'

'Good girls.' Luca straightened and Polly met his gaze, her heart turning over as he winked at her. 'Let's go and meet Georgina.'

As they approached the yard office, a young woman came out and told them that Georgina was on the telephone and would be out to greet them shortly. Polly used the few moments to look around her. There had been considerable improvements and upgrading since her last visit, but the core of the place was the same, and memories swamped her.

The yard was busy and Polly remembered what it had been like to work here. How she'd missed these surroundings… being around the horses, even mucking out stables and cleaning tack. If she closed her eyes she could almost capture the familiar scents of leather and saddle soap and neastsfoot oil.

'All right?'

Polly turned and met Luca's intense dark gaze, seeing the concern for her in the depths of his eyes. She hadn't been sure how she would feel revisiting what had been her sanctuary and escape, but… Releasing a shaky breath, she nodded and managed a smile.

'I'm fine.'

Luca held her gaze a moment longer, then nodded, apparently satisfied.

'I'm sorry to keep you waiting, Dr d'Azzaro. I won't be a second.'

Georgie's voice, long unheard and yet familiar, came from inside the office. Feeling nervous, excited, unsure, Polly missed Luca's reply. Her thoughts were on Georgina. They hadn't been friends, exactly. Polly hadn't had any friends. But Georgina had been the closest to one she'd. Outgoing, self-assured and popular, Georgina had always been kind to her, seeming to understand her need to be around the horses and making her feel welcome as she spent all the time she could there, doing any chores assigned her and earning herself the occasional ride or lesson which she could never otherwise have afforded.

As Georgina stepped out of the office, her attention was focused on Luca and the children. It gave Polly a moment to study her former classmate who was dressed in the ubiquitous jodhpurs, riding boots and a sweatshirt with the riding stable's monogram on the front. Of average height, Georgina was slim but curvy, with shoulder-length, burnished brown hair and hazel eyes. She certainly didn't look thirteen years older, Polly thought.

'We'll have a look round and introduce you to some ponies to see how you feel, and then we can discuss what you'd like to do riding-wise,' Georgina suggested, smiling as the twins beamed and clapped their hands with glee.

'That sounds good, thank you,' Luca agreed.

Nodding, Georgina turned and looked at Polly, then did a double-take, surprise, disbelief and, finally, delight, crossing her face. 'My, God! Polly…is that really you?'

'Hello, Georgie.' Polly's throat felt thick with emotion.

Georgie closed the gap between them and enveloped her in a hug. 'Oh, it's so good to see you! You look great—barely a day older, damn you! And so pretty,' she enthused, stepping back a pace to look at her.

'Oh, I'm just the same old me,' Polly dismissed, her smile faltering. 'You, however, look amazing.'

'Thanks. Luka adds the sparkle—' She broke off and giggled as she looked at them. 'My husband, I mean. Luka with a "k"!' she explained, making them laugh with her and at the same time demonstrating the subtle difference in pronunciation between the two men's names.

'How are your parents?' Polly asked.

'They're well, thanks for asking.' Georgie's smile was mischievous. 'It took Dad a while to let go and get used to retirement—and to me marrying Luka—but he's fine now.'

Malcolm Somers had run things with military precision, his fingers on the pulse of everything that went on, and Polly found it hard to imagine him relaxing.

'They'll be so delighted to have news of you,' Georgie said, surprising her anew. 'We all missed you. Oh, Polly, I had no idea where you'd gone or how to contact you. And I must admit I feared you might never come back,' she told her, giving her another brief hug. 'We must arrange to meet and have a really good talk—we have so much to catch up on. OK?'

Polly nodded. It would be good to rekindle a friendship with bubbly, generous Georgie—one of the few people who had been kind to her and of whom she had good memories from the past. 'I'd like that.'

'Excellent! As for now, would you like to have a walk around and explore? We've made a few changes in the last couple of years.' A glint appeared in Georgie's eyes. 'Do you remember where Long Meadow is?' she asked, and Polly nodded. 'Well, you might enjoy a walk down there, too.'

Knowing Polly needed some time alone, Luca reluctantly watched her walk away, then turned his attention to his excited daughters and the purpose of their visit here, following Georgina and the girls into the office for a chat.

'Three, nearly four isn't too young to begin riding lessons?' Luca asked, keen to assess the woman who might well be in charge of the safety of his children.

'It's never too young to learn to ride—or swim.' Georgina smiled and looked at the girls. 'My father will tell you I was doing both before I could walk! But it very much depends on the child, too. I don't believe in forcing anyone, but I do believe in supporting and encouraging those who have a natural aptitude or who clearly enjoy it and benefit from it. And it is very soon apparent which children fall into which group.'

Luca nodded, liking her answer. 'Rosie and Toni have been talking ponies for some time. I thought it best to wait and see how they get on before investing in hats and boots and things of their own.'

'Very sensible. We have everything they need to begin with.' She called one of her stable girls, who found the right-sized hats for the twins. Georgina smiled, curiosity in her eyes. 'It's fantastic to see Polly. How long has she been back in Cornwall?'

'Since July, but from what I understand it has been difficult for her, so don't be too hard on her for not coming to see you before,' he suggested gently, seeing the play of emotions across Georgina's expressive face.

'No. You're right. As I said, I never expected to see her again. It must have taken a lot for her to come back here. Why did she? What is she doing?'

'Polly is a GP—an excellent one—and she is working at the Penhally surgery, like me. We only met two weeks ago, but I know she came here when she was young and things were difficult at home.'

'I felt sad for her. There were rumours and stories about Reg Searle—his drinking, his gambling, his inability to hold down a job or care properly for Polly. She was always so lonely and unhappy,' Georgina confirmed, breaking Luca's heart anew. 'She kept so much to herself, always in the background, losing herself in her books. When she started coming here and clearly enjoyed it, my parents and I did all we could to encourage her. My mother worried constantly that she was so thin, and we wanted to draw her into the family, at least to feed her, but we were afraid of driving her away, depriving her of the very thing she needed.'

Luca watched as Georgina rose to her feet and crossed to a large pinboard, which held hundreds of photos of horses, ponies and riders. Unerringly her hand went to one in particular and she took it down, smiling as she turned around.

'Polly had one special friend here. I never let on that I knew, or broke her confidence, but I often heard her pouring out her heart to him. It nearly broke mine.'

'Him?' Luca experienced an uncomfortable moment of jealousy.

Georgina handed him the photo and he looked down, seeing a thin little girl with untidy long blonde hair, her arms wrapped round the neck of a chestnut pony. 'Polly...' He could see the loneliness in her eyes, and if he thought she was tiny now, she had been like a little waif when this photo had been taken.

'Polly was about thirteen then. The pony, Copper Canyon, was five. I know because my father bought a lovely Irish mare, not knowing she was in foal, and Copper was born on my eighth birthday and given to me. I saw how Polly bonded with him and was happy to share.'

'Thank you for being such a good friend to her,' he said, his voice rough.

'Copper's twenty-two now, and retired from any riding-school duties.'

Luca realised the significance for Polly. 'But he's here?'

'Yes.' Georgina's smile was wide. 'That's why I sent her down to Long Meadow. I'd love to see her face when she finds him!'

So would he, Luca admitted to himself, as much to make sure Polly was all right as anything else. She had been through a great deal of emotional turmoil in the last few days and he was full of admiration for her courage and resilience, coping with each new surprise while still coming to terms with her past.

The weekend had been both heaven and hell. It was purgatory having Polly in his bed, snuggled up against him and wrapped in his arms. He could breathe in her scent—lilac mingling with her sweet femininity—feel her warmth and fragility, the beat of her heart, but not to be able to touch, kiss and make love to her as he so wanted to was driving him crazy. He had to slip from the bed each morning before she became aware of his aroused state. And he was fed up with cold showers. Yet on the two nights they had been together, he had slept better than he had in years.

Polly was also overcoming whatever hesitancy she had first exhibited with Rosie and Toni. That the twins loved her was obvious, and he thought back to last night when they had begged for her to put them to bed. Polly had looked startled, unsure, and he had feared she would say no, but she had agreed. After clearing up following the night-time bath ritual, he'd stood outside the girls' room, leaning against the wall. Polly had been a revelation, and he'd discovered a whole new side to her, one which had seen his growing love for her expand even more.

It had been Toni's turn to select a story and true to form it had both animals and an adventure in it. Polly had surprised and delighted him, displaying a natural gift for storytelling, getting involved and putting on different voices for all the characters. He hadn't been able to tear himself away, enchanted by this fun side of her soft and gentle nature. The story finished, he'd peeped into the room, and his heart had clenched at the sight of both his girls cuddled up against Polly on Toni's bed as she had stroked their hair.

'Mamma died when we were born.'

Rosie's sleepy words drifted to him and he drew back, holding his breath as he waited for Polly's reply.

'I know, darling, and I'm so sorry,' Polly soothed.

'Papà said she had to go to heaven,' Rosie added, and

although it hurt, Luca was relieved there was acceptance, not distress in his daughter's voice.

'My mother died when I was very young, too, so I know how it feels. But you and Toni are blessed to have Papà. He loves you so much, and he'll always be there for you, encouraging you to reach for your dreams and sheltering you from harm.'

Luca had no idea if the girls had heard all Polly's words because by the time she had finished speaking, they were asleep. But he had heard them. And it took a few moments to ease the lump that had formed in his throat. He had felt so humbled that Polly believed him to be a good father but there had also been the painful knowledge of everything Polly had lacked, that as a child she'd been deprived of the love and care and cherishing she had deserved. He hoped it wasn't too late to give her those things, because with every day that passed, he was more and more sure that he wanted her in his life…for all his life.

With Polly, he felt the most amazing closeness and inti-macy, and a real sense of peace. It was extraordinary how far he had come in two weeks, from meeting Polly, fighting against the initial desire and not wanting any involvement with a woman to now…unable to bear a moment apart from her, knowing something very special was happening that could make a huge difference to his future and that of his children.

He also knew there were issues yet to be discussed that Polly needed to face before she was free to embrace that future with him.

'You can keep the photo,' Georgina said now, drawing him from his thoughts. She hesitated, then she glanced up and met his gaze, a serious expression in her hazel eyes. 'I'm only mentioning this because of the way Polly responded when I complimented her on how she looked.'

'Go on,' Luca invited, his attention sharpening. He, too, had noted Polly's dismissive denial, especially as it had come so soon after her rejection of Jane's comment about her sharing her mother's looks.

'I know Polly doesn't have a copy of this picture, because I offered her one at the time and she wouldn't take it.'

Luca frowned. 'Why not?'

'She said it would cause trouble if her father found it and she didn't want to risk her visits here to the stables,' Georgina admitted, and he felt sick to his stomach at the implications. 'She gave it back to me and said she'd written a suitable caption on the back. It's what Reg called her.'

Something in the young woman's voice forewarned Luca that he wouldn't like what he was about to see. Slowly, he turned the photograph over, his gaze zeroing in on the four words written in a youthful but recognisable hand. Plain Polly from Penhally. *Dio!* He could only imagine the damage caused by the planting of those words in Polly's mind when she was so young and fragile—words he feared the man who had dared to call himself her father would have repeated insidiously, and, from all he had learned so far, with perverse enjoyment, knowing it would hurt.

To judge from all Polly had said, and her problems with the anorexia, she had believed those words. Did she still? Was that what lay behind her lack of self-belief and the way she hid her body? Was that why she rejected any suggestions that she was attractive and desirable? He needed to find out. Because if it was, it was way past time he did something about it.

'Maybe Polly would like a copy of the picture now,' Georgina suggested.

Luca nodded. 'Thanks. I'll take care of it.'

'No...thank *you*,' she countered with emphasis.

Luca raised an eyebrow in surprise. 'Me?'

'Yes. For bringing Polly back here...' She paused a moment, watching him. 'And gut instinct tells me you're just what Polly needs. Look after her, Dr d'Azzaro.'

'I plan to. If she'll let me. And it's Luca…with a "c",' he added, making her laugh.

Still chuckling, Georgina rose to her feet. 'OK, girls, shall we get started and take you for your first ride?'

Following through the yard, his heart swelled in his chest as he watched his daughters almost burst with joy as they met their first real-life pony. He loved them so much. They were his life. But he still found it hard to reconcile what Elaine had done…and how she had done it. If things were to go much further, he needed to know that Polly would never try to do the same. There was an issue with her and children, that was obvious, and it was one more important thing he needed to understand. Soon.

The changes and improvements Georgina and Luka were making to the riding stables were obvious, and everything about the yard seemed more professional and run to an even higher standard. After looking round the new indoor school, Polly went back outside and paused for a moment to watch the lesson under way in one of the ménages. The horses and ponies were in excellent condition, and all the staff, including volunteers as she had been, were smart and wearing monogrammed sweatshirts like the one Georgina had on.

As Polly walked down between the well-fenced paddocks, some of which were being rested, while others contained animals enjoying good-quality grazing, the late September sun was warm on her skin. Occasional trees lined the track, providing pockets of shade, and Polly stepped into one of these when she reached Long Meadow, an attractive field bordered by woods and which had a shallow stream flowing through it.

Folding her arms on the top of the post-and-rail fence,

Polly sighed, letting the memories roll over her. Her gaze moved over the half-dozen ponies in the field before her, settled on one and stopped.

'No…it can't be.' The words whispered from her as she stared in disbelief at the chestnut gelding grazing a short distance away. 'Copper?' She shook her head, her heart thudding in her chest as she raised her voice and called again, loudly this time. 'Copper!'

The pony's head came up and turned in her direction. She called his name once more, hardly daring to believe it was true, but a soft whicker sounded in answer and the pony began to walk towards her. Copper Canyon, her special friend! He must be in his twenties, she calculated, amazed and delighted to see how well he looked. Surely it was fanciful to believe he remembered her after thirteen years apart? Yet there was no denying the way he was responding to her voice. And Georgina must have known…she had deliberately sent her down here.

He arrived before her, his head over the fence, ears pricked, eyes alert. 'Oh, Copper,' she whispered, tears escaping as she wrapped her arms around him and buried her face in the silken warmth of his neck.

There was nothing like the smell of horse. Polly closed her eyes and inhaled the familiar, comforting scent, feeling some of her tension melting away. She ran her fingers through Copper's mane and along the muscled curve of his neck, and it was as if thirteen years had been stripped away. He'd been her only real friend. Time and again she had poured out her heart to him, sobbing out her pain and despair about Reg, her hopes and dreams for the future.

She drew back a little, stroking his face, rubbing the spot at the base of his ear, just as he had always loved, enjoying the softness of his muzzle as he explored her face and neck. All too soon he moved a few steps away and began to graze again. She missed the immediate contact but basked in the joy of their reunion.

'Are you all right, *zingarella*?'

With a startled gasp, Polly swung round to find Luca close behind her, recalling too late the evidence of her tears. 'Yes… thanks.'

'And the tears, they are happy ones at seeing your special friend?' he asked, stepping even closer, making her supremely aware of him.

Polly nodded, unable to force out any words as Luca's hands cupped her face, the pads of his thumbs erasing the moisture from her cheeks. 'The girls?'

'Are in their element and loving every moment,' he confirmed. 'They want you to see them.'

'OK.'

There was something different about him. Polly couldn't explain what it was, but every part of her responded to it, the aching knot deep inside tightening and every nerve-ending tingling as his fingers continued to caress her face, slowly moving down to her throat, and then lower, whispering along her collar bones. He leaned in, his lips nibbling along her jawline to her ear, teasing her lobe before his tongue tickled the sensitive hollow beneath. A shudder rippled through her.

'Luca?' she whispered, a curious mix of uncertainty and excitement building inside her, her legs feeling too unsteady to hold her upright. 'What is it?'

He looked up and her breath caught at the sultry, slow burn heat in deep brown eyes. 'There's been a change of plan.' Another step closer and his body made contact with hers, gently rubbing against her, firing her blood and liquefying her bones with the full-body caress.

'W-What do you mean?' she stammered.

'I mean, *mio amore*, that I cannot allow another day to end with you believing you are unattractive and undesirable.' His thumb brushed across her trembling lower lip. 'So I'm taking you home to prove to you how beautiful and sexy you are.'

CHAPTER NINE

By the time they left the stables after the twins' first successful riding experience, Polly had convinced herself that she had misunderstood Luca's shocking pronouncement. More of her tension eased on the journey back to Penhally until, that was, Luca made an unexpected stop at the deserted surgery.

'I will be just a moment.'

True to his word, he was back in a very short time, although he didn't appear to be carrying anything. Polly, her stomach fluttering uneasily, couldn't help but be curious about what he was up to, but as he slid behind the wheel, their gazes met, and the sultry expression in deep, dark eyes sucked all the air from her lungs. OK...so maybe it was safer for her not to know.

She had hardly regained her breath when they made another unscheduled stop. Polly had no idea how or when Luca had arranged it—or what reason he had given—but the twins were to spend some time with Oliver and Chloe. Delighted at the prospect of playing with Chloe's cats and meeting up with Gabriel and Lauren to walk Foxy, Rosie and Toni ran off without a backward glance.

Left alone with Luca, Polly felt the tension ratchet up on the final mile back to Keeper's Cottage. Every part of her seemed electrified, from the top of her head to the tips of her toes, whereas Luca, damn him, appeared composed and unruffled. Exactly what he had in mind for them Polly wasn't sure, but her imagination was racing at a million miles an hour. And now they were home and she was running out of time.

'Luca,' she murmured, desperate need, fear, excitement and anxiety just some of the emotions churning inside her as he took her hand and led her up the stairs to his bedroom. 'I'm not at all sure about this.'

'I'm very sure.'

How could he be? Her heart was threatening to beat right out of her chest and she felt paralysed with nerves as Luca moved around the room, turning down the duvet, removing his watch, his shoes and socks. He then took a packet of condoms from his pocket and set it on the bedside table. She swallowed back a rush of fearful excitement, realising now what the impromptu stop at the surgery had been for.

Colour tinging her cheeks, Polly could only stare as Luca's fingers moved to the buttons of his shirt and slowly, slowly began to undo them. She had seen him wearing less on the beach, and in the last couple of days—had slept *with him*, in this very bed, with only a couple of thin layers of material between them. But this was different. *Luca* was different. He'd changed the rules. And now… Oh, my!

He slid off his shirt and tossed it aside in a gesture of thoughtless abandon, as if all that mattered was to be rid of it, revealing all that smooth, olive skin and rippling muscle. Next he turned his attention to his belt, unfastening it and sliding it free from the loops at the waistband of his jeans, letting it fall where it may. His wallet came next, drawn from his back pocket and set on the nearby chest. The snap of the button and parting of the teeth of the zip sounded unnaturally loud in the silence of the room and Polly fought for each ragged breath, unable to move or to look away as he eased out of the jeans. Dressed only now in boxer shorts, he closed the gap between them.

Luca had the most incredible physique. Her mouth watered as her gaze devoured him, moving from his strong shoulders down to his broad chest and six-pack abdomen, the covering of dark hair she itched to feel that arrowed down in a tantalising line over his navel and disappearing beneath his boxer shorts.

He halted in front of her…so close that the warm, musky aroma of him teased her senses, heightening her arousal and clouding her thoughts. One of her hands lifted, and it took a supreme effort of will to resist the temptation to explore.

'You can touch,' he invited, his voice warm and low and sexy as he caught her hand and drew her palm to rest over his heart, near the tattoo bearing the twins' names, where she could feel its steady if rapid beat. 'I long to feel your hands on my body.'

His words made her hot all over, her pulse racing as she imagined having the freedom to do just that. For now she was preoccupied with savouring the feel of warm male skin and discovering that the dark hair on his chest was silkier than she had expected…so much so that she was scarcely aware of Luca picking up his wallet and taking something out.

'Do you remember this, *zingarella*?' he asked softly.

Polly was shocked to find herself looking at an old photograph of her in her early teens with Copper. 'Yes. I remember.'

'Georgina gave it to me. She said you wouldn't keep it all those years ago, but she thought you might like a copy now,' Luca explained, and Polly cursed the sting of tears that pricked her eyes as old memories and emotions flooded her.

'Th-Thank you.'

'Do you also remember writing on the back?'

Something in his tone alerted her and her gaze clashed with his. Dark eyes were filled with compassion and implacable determination. She looked back at the photo, seeing the scruffy, painfully thin little girl she had been, and briefly closed her eyes. What had she written? She didn't know.

Luca turned the picture over. For a moment Polly couldn't bring herself to look. When she did, an involuntary sound escaped, somewhere between a gasp and a sob. She averted her gaze, humiliated that Luca knew the words that resonated in her brain now, just as they had done for over twenty-five years…*Plain Polly from Penhally.*

'Those were Reg's words?' Luca asked, refusing to bestow the title 'father' on the man, and hoping for Polly's sake that the anger banked inside him was masked.

'Yes.'

The word whispered out on a sigh, but it was the shame, resignation and hurt in her blue eyes that cut him into pieces. 'This morning, when Jane said you looked like your mother, you denied it. Why?'

'My mother was beautiful. I know I'm not,' she riposted, lashes lowering to hide her expression. Her voice was thick and low when she spoke again. 'I've always known what I am.'

'And what do you think you are, *zingarella*?'

'The anorexia took its toll. And Rex was right…so was Charles, my ex-husband.' She paused a moment, and he felt a shudder ripple through her. 'I'm unfeminine, scrawny and unattractive.'

Luca had never known that silence could be so loud before, but as each second passed and neither of them spoke, Luca's anger roared in his ears, growing to fever-pitch—anger at the man who had dared to call himself a father and who had conditioned Polly from such a young age to feel so bad about herself. At the moment the information about her marriage was sketchy, but he very much wanted to know about her husband, Charles. From what she had just said, the man had failed to make Polly feel loved and cherished. If Luca had his way he would be telling—and showing—her every day for the rest of their lives how beautiful and loved and special she was. Starting now.

'Come with me.'

Luca knew he was taking a risk, but he believed he had to do it, that it was time…for both of them. He could feel Polly shaking as he led her across the room to the full-length mirror, placing her in front of it and standing up close behind her. Wrapping one arm loosely around her waist, he cupped her chin with his free hand and raised her head until their gazes locked in the mirror.

'You are a beautiful woman, Polly.' He saw the immediate denial and disbelief in her eyes, but he was determined to counteract them. 'Your skin is flawless, peachy-soft, so touchable,' he told her, hearing the huskiness of his voice as he began his honest assessment of her. His fingers caressed the line of her jaw before moving on the trace all the features of her face. 'The contrast of your pale skin against mine fascinates me. Your bone structure is exquisite.'

'L-Luca…'

He shushed her interruption, continuing to hold her gaze in the mirror, feeling her response to his touch and his words in the tremble of her body, the faint wash of colour across her cheeks, the unsteadiness of her breathing and the increasingly rapid beat of her heart.

'Your eyes, glinting like dark sapphires, mesmerise me,' he continued, using one finger to lightly trace her brows, before moving on down. 'This is so cute!' He smiled as he gently tweaked the tip of her small, straight nose. She was following his every move, he could see, confusion mingling with doubt and growing desire. He brushed the pad of his thumb across the swell of her lips, which parted instantly.

'And as for your mouth…if I don't kiss you properly, very soon, I shall go crazy. Your lips are so soft, so sexy. I want to taste you, to unleash the burning passion we've both been trying hard to keep in check since we met. I want you, Polly. I want to see all of you, kiss all of you, spend hours making love with you.'

A whimper escaped her, a needy little sound that aroused him even more, and as she leaned back into him for support, he splayed his hand low over her belly to hold her close as he rubbed his hips against the delicate curve of her bottom, letting her know just how hard he was for her.

'Can you feel how much I want you?' he murmured against her ear, teasing the lobe between his lips before sucking on it, teasing her as her breath hitched and she swayed against him. 'You, Polly. For the first time since Elaine died, I'm attracted to a woman. It is *you* I respond to, you I find attractive and beautiful.'

His fingers moved to the zip of her fleece, opening it before easing it from her shoulders and dropping it to the floor. As his fingers moved to the buttons of the shirt she wore beneath it, he watched her reactions in the mirror. Her body tensed as he undid one button at a time and disposed of the shirt. The final layer was a sleeveless white crop top. The cotton fabric clung to her body and revealed that she was not wearing a bra. Aroused, swollen nipples were clearly defined, cresting the small globes of her breasts. He couldn't wait another moment to touch her, his palms covering her through the soft fabric and gently shaping her firm flesh.

Polly moaned, her head dropping back against his shoulder as her body arched to his caresses. Impatient, his hands gathered the material, pulling it up, and she raised her arms to allow him to remove it, but dropped them to cover herself, her face flushed in the reflection of the mirror, uncertainty returning to her eyes.

He whispered his fingertips up her arms and across her collar bones, feeling her quiver. 'Why do you wear all these clothes to hide your figure, *mio amore*?'

'I haven't got a figure…not like Chloe and Lauren and Gemma,' she whispered.

'You most certainly have.' Taking his time, he gently eased her arms from across her chest, every part of her shaking as he stroked her abdomen, slowly working up until his fingers shaped the outline of her breasts, zeroing in to the swollen dusky-pink nipples that crested them. 'You're beautiful… small but perfectly formed.'

To his surprise and consternation, even as her body responded instinctively to his touch and his hands slid down to unfasten her jeans, tears filled her eyes. 'You don't understand.'

'I know you hate your body and it cuts me up inside that you cannot see what I see…that you are lovely and special and desirable,' he answered, his lips skimming kisses across her bare shoulder. 'Let me show you, Polly. Let me love you.'

'I have a scar.' Her voice broke. Unable to bear it any more, he turned her in his arms and gathered her close. 'There are things I need to tell you that might change your mind.'

He cupped her face, thumbs brushing the moisture from her cheeks. 'Nothing will change my mind and a scar is not going to put me off,' he reassured her.

'It's afternoon,' she protested weakly as he backed her towards the bed. 'The curtains…'

'No one can see in. And I want to see you. Just as I want to make love to you at any time of day,' he teased, working deftly on the fastening of her jeans and brushing them and her tiny lace panties down her legs. He couldn't help but see the scar low on her abdomen or know from its size and position that a painful story lay behind it, but he wanted her reassured before she told him. 'Do you think I am not nervous, too, *zingarella*? Do you think I am not scared?'

Sapphire-blue eyes widened. 'You? But why?'

'I've not kissed or touched a woman in nearly four years—have not done anything with anyone but Elaine since the day I met her. What if I disappoint you? It's scary starting over with someone new.' He saw her surprise, but laid out his own insecurities for her to see. His hands gently caressed her. She was so fragile he feared she might snap if he held her too tightly or made love to her with the fiery passion churning inside him. 'You're so beautiful, so slender... What if I hurt you?'

Polly was stunned as she listened to Luca's fears. She had no doubt they were genuine and that he had them at all, that he could doubt himself, eased some of her own worries. There were things she had to tell him. He said now they wouldn't matter, but what if they did? What if she told him first and it *did* put him off, and then she never knew what it would be like to make love with him? She was scared, of so many things, including what might happen afterwards, but whatever happened, she had to grasp this moment—in case it was the only one she ever had.

Filled with an uncharacteristic boldness, her hands returned to his body, her fingers tracing the corded muscles of his arms, feeling his strength, the hard muscle under warm, smooth skin. She lightly dragged her nails down his chest, through the soft, springy hair, gaining confidence as he groaned, dark eyes heavy lidded with pleasure and passion. Unable to wait another moment, she stepped up and pressed her body against him, satisfying the need to feel his chest against her own, his hair an exciting caress against her soft skin and peaked nipples that hardened even further as she rubbed herself against him.

Every millimetre of her skin was on fire from the caress of his hands exploring her own body and she was trembling from head to toe, frustrated that she couldn't get close enough. She looked up, the hollow ache inside her intensifying at the primal look in his dark eyes.

Their mouths met, no longer with soft, gentle, safe kisses. For the first time, this was the real thing and instantly the passion ignited, exploded, enveloping them both in its blazing intensity. Polly could do nothing but surrender herself to it, lost in something extraordinary and which she had never experienced before. Neither of them had allowed the desire to take hold before, but now the passion that had simmered just beneath the surface from the first moment they had met burst free—like the eruption of a volcano blowing its top when the pressure within, building and building, could no longer be contained. It rocked her to her toes. It excited her beyond bearing. And it scared her to death.

Despite the urgency, she could sense Luca holding onto the last threads of his control. 'I want to savour every part of you,' he mouthed against her skin as they fell to the bed.

True to his word, his hands and his mouth drove her to near insanity as he explored every part of her body, making her feel cherished for the first time in her life, treating her with such care, and overwhelming her with the intensity of his kisses and caresses, the sinful and inventive exploits of his hands and mouth. She explored in turn, revelling in the freedom to learn all the different textures and tastes of his body.

She froze when he touched her scar with his fingers. And when he traced it with his lips, bestowing the softest, sweetest kisses, it made her cry. He was so special, so caring, and despite not knowing its cause, he'd sensed its importance to her and without words was accepting it as part of her. As if he had all the time in the world, he kissed his way up to her navel and Polly gasped. She heard Luca chuckle as she squirmed against him, warm breath tickling her skin. She'd had no idea she was so sensitive there and was still savouring the sensations when his mouth reached one of her breasts. She cried out as lips, teeth and tongue tormented supersensitive flesh before drawing her nipple into his mouth and sucking strongly, making her sob at the almost unbearable pleasure as he rolled and teased her nipple between his tongue and the roof of his mouth.

Her whole body was on fire and she needed him to fill the emptiness, to take away the terrible ache deep inside her, and she needed him to do it *now*. No more waiting. But he was holding back and Polly was worried it was because of the fears he had voiced. She slid her hands up his arms, feeling the tension in them as he supported his weight. Her fingers curled into taut biceps as she urged him to let go.

'Luca, please.'

'I don't want to hurt you.'

'You won't. I'm not going to break. I need you, need this.' She buried her face in his neck, nibbling and licking his skin, breathing in the intoxicating musky male scent of him. 'All of you. Now. *Please...*'

He groaned, and she felt the shudder run through him. Looking into his eyes, she saw the passion in them, the need, and she knew the moment he gave up the struggle for control. She knew a surge of excitement, a flicker of nervousness and a sense of feminine triumph, and then she couldn't think of anything at all but the new explosion of passion that swept them both away, whirling her into something more intimate and intense and extraordinary than she had ever imagined possible.

She welcomed the press of his body on hers and she arched up, seeking more, wrapping her legs around him, her cry mingling with his in reaction to the joyful intensity as their bodies became one with a single fluid motion. Her mouth met his in a searing kiss that stole what little breath she had left. Luca fisted the fingers of one hand in her hair, his other arm sliding under her hips to lock her to him.

It was as if their bodies recognised each other, were made for each other, moving in an age-old rhythm, immediate, demanding, out of control. Making love with Luca unleashed hidden, untapped depths of her own sensuality she had not known existed, but she threw herself into the moment, losing herself in the magical connection between them, meeting his demands and making demands of her own. They drove each other higher and higher. Polly never wanted this incredible experience to end, but she couldn't hold on any longer. She pleaded with him, her hands dragging at him as she tried to get ever closer, and they clung together as their pleasure crested, crying out as they spun together, freefalling into the abyss, the ecstasy indescribable.

Luca had taken her to paradise and, at that moment, she didn't care if she ever came back to earth again.

Days turned into weeks, and the end of summer morphed into a warm, wet autumn. While the bond between herself and Luca strengthened every day, and she was drawn ever more deeply into the d'Azzaro family, Polly became increasingly scared that she wasn't allowed to be this happy. Any time soon something would burst her bubble of joyful contentment and smash her back to earth with a bump.

Professionally, things had been hectic, Penhally Bay Surgery continuing to draw in new patients as the services offered expanded. The Saturday clinic for young people was busier than ever and Luca's help with the youngsters was invaluable. His presence also gave her confidence to tackle the cases she found most difficult…those of young people coming to her with issues that mirrored those she had faced in her own life.

Kate had returned to work at the beginning of the month and Polly was relieved to see the older woman regain her strength and vitality. Speculation was rife that Rob would ask Kate to marry him, but Polly remained silent. Kate had said nothing, but Polly suspected that her friend would want to wait until her hospital appointment in January when she would hopefully hear that the cancer had gone. The only discordant note was the ongoing tension between Kate and Nick, and Polly had no idea how that issue was ever going to be resolved.

Polly cherished the time she spent with Rosie and Toni, reading to them, teaching them to bake cookies and muffins, playing with them and enjoying their unbounded joy about the puppy. Little Jasper had been with them for almost two weeks now, a glossy black bundle of fun and mischief who had won all their hearts. The girls were wonderful with him, attentive and caring and determined to do as much for him themselves as they could.

Chloe's idea of a puppy crèche had proved invaluable. Dragan and Melinda had kept one puppy for themselves, a boy called Cocoa. Nick's niece, Charlotte, newly engaged to James, had taken a black boy called Dylan. Jem's puppy was called Bruno, Oliver and Chloe's Rolo, and Gabriel and Lauren's Monet, after Lauren's favourite painter. It was sometimes chaotic but always enjoyable and while serving to help the puppies to learn and grow, the shared experience was tightening the bonds of friendship between the humans, too.

As the end of October approached, Polly couldn't believe how much her life had changed—how much *she* had changed. It hadn't all been easy, but Luca had been beside her every step of the way as she had faced the remaining demons from her past, just as she had tried to be supportive of him as he had lain the final threads of Elaine's ghost to rest.

Sitting at her desk in her consulting room with a rare few moments alone, Polly stared out of the window as another shower fizzled out and the sky began to lighten. For the first time in four years she was coping with this time of year, able to face Halloween with her own personal horror less raw. Thanks to Luca. That amazing Sunday afternoon a month ago when they had first made love had been as memorable for the things they had talked about afterwards as for the extraordinary physical connection they had shared. Polly would never forget it…

'Whatever happens between us in the days and weeks ahead, I want you to know that I will never lie to you,' Luca had told her, cradling her in his arms. 'And I ask you to promise me the same.'

Polly had nodded, taken aback by the serious tone of his voice. 'OK.'

'It's important to me, Polly.'

'I can see that.' She had wondered why. 'What happened to make you feel so strongly about this?'

He had paused a moment, his smile fading, dark eyes filling with changing emotions, including pain and anger. His voice had been controlled when he had spoken, as if trying to cover the turmoil within him. 'Elaine wanted a baby so badly that she tricked me with the pregnancy and kept the truth from me about the risk to herself if she carried a baby to full term. She knew there was a high probability she would die, leaving me alone with an infant baby, but she didn't tell me until near the end, until there was no choice left for me. She said she was afraid I would have tried to change her mind. Of course I would. I loved her. The idea of a baby—at that point unknown and unformed—to me was not worth the risk of losing Elaine. Part of me is still angry with her—both for taking the decision alone, and for leaving me and the girls—and yet had she not done it Rosie and Toni would not be here. But how can you ask any man to make that kind of choice?'

'I don't know. You can't. You shouldn't have to. It was awful, but not your fault, Luca.' She had shifted position, hugging him, pressing kisses to the strong column of his throat. 'Elaine was very wrong to deceive you. Some might say she was selfish, knowing she might well be committing her child to life without a mother, not to mention the impact on you. Others might say it was the ultimate sacrifice—she wanted a baby with you so badly that she felt it worth that risk.'

His fingers in her hair, he tilted her head so he could meet her gaze, the pain in his eyes taking her breath away. 'I can't go through anything like that again, Polly. I know there is something about the girls that makes you sad when you look at them. Is it because of this?' he asked softly, the fingers of his free hand inexorably finding and tracing the line of her scar.

'Yes.'

Emotion welling inside her, Polly sucked in a ragged breath, knowing the time had come for her to step off the precipice and tell Luca everything, hoping he would catch her.

And so it all came pouring out. How, after a couple of short-lived and unsatisfactory dating experiences, she met Charles Atkinson as she neared the end of medical school. Two years her senior and a trainee surgeon, he was the first person, besides Kate, to show her any kind of affection and, looking back, she realised now that that had helped to skew her judgement.

'Charles was smart and good-looking, sophisticated, and a lot of the female staff vied for his attention. I couldn't believe it when he said he was interested in me,' she explained, a squeeze of pain tightening inside her as the old Plain Polly from Penhally taunt whispered through her mind. 'He was kind, patient, apparently prepared not to rush me into anything, and I lapped up the attention.'

'I'm not surprised after you had been starved of it for so long,' Luca soothed.

'Eventually we become lovers. He was the first person I'd been intimate with and while he didn't set my whole world on fire, I enjoyed being with him, and I was so caught up in the whole thing, surprised anyone might care about me, that I didn't realise how little I really knew about him.' She paused, trying to gather her thoughts. 'Charles was very ambitious and managed to land a much-coveted place on the team of a renowned surgeon on Harley Street. He had an almost obsessive zeal to succeed, and I thought he understood why my own career was important to me.'

Luca's fingers stroked her hair. 'But he didn't?'

'As it turned out, no, but I didn't see it then,' she confided with a frown.

'What happened?'

'To cut a long story short, we got married after I qualified. It was a very quiet, no-frills registry office wedding—neither of us had family, Kate couldn't come up to London at that time, and so there were just a couple of Charles's work friends as witnesses.' A shiver rippled through her as the memories returned. 'At first things were OK, then Charles began making comments about me giving up work and starting a family. We'd discussed it, and I'd told him I didn't want children, probably ever.' Her voice wavered and she hesitated, trying to get it back under control. 'I had this thing in my head that I was never going to pass on Reg's genes. I didn't want to one day look at my child and see him looking back at me.'

Luca tightened his hold and dropped a kiss on her forehead. 'I can understand that.' The sincerity in his voice reassured her.

'I wasn't unhappy that first year and I loved my work. The changes began gradually, insidiously. Little things at first. Almost unnoticeable. Charles started to criticise the way I looked, the way I kept the home, then he complained that I worked too much. His personality began to change, too, and he became impatient, tired and irritable. Nothing was right. He was drinking more and spending hours on the computer. He was secretive and angry when I questioned him, and he told me it was work and none of my business. I started to get scared, fearing Charles was showing some of the signs I'd known too well in Reg.

'Things got worse as the months progressed,' she continued, unconsciously snuggling into Luca, seeking comfort and security as she told him things she had never told anyone else. 'Charles became more critical, more inconsistent in his behaviour and more and more determined I give up work. He wanted to be the successful one and he was determined his wife should be at home, doing his bidding, making him look good. And, he said, his job was more important than mine. I refused and we argued all the time as he became increasingly controlling.'

Polly felt Luca tense. 'Did he hurt you?' he demanded roughly.

'Not physically. Not then…'

'*Dio!* Polly, what did he do?' Luca demanded, his concern for her giving her the strength to go on, to face the worst yet to come.

'We rarely made love any more, and I was glad, because when we did he was selfish, taking only what he wanted. I didn't know what to do. I'd taken my vows seriously, and the way he was wearing down my self-esteem was just like Reg, until I thought it must be my fault, that I wasn't good enough. At the beginning I'd agreed to a joint bank account, but soon he was using that to control me, to make sure I had to ask for any money I wanted. I thought of opening my own account and to switch having my salary paid into that, but Charles

ound the forms before I could finalise things and went mad.
t was around then that Reg died. I didn't want anything from
im, but I'd confided some of my problems to Kate, and when
a firm of will hunters contacted her, Kate put them in touch
with me. I was Reg's only heir. The value of the house was
all that was left, and Kate persuaded me to swallow my pride
and to take Reg's money, to put it in a safe place Charles knew
nothing about in case I ever needed an escape route.'

'It was good advice.' Luca kissed her, his voice gentle.
'And then what happened?'

Polly closed her eyes, remembering. 'I discovered I was
pregnant. I was shocked and upset, more so when Charles
admitted he had deliberately tampered with my birth control.
We rowed terribly for weeks, it seemed. The timing was
wrong, I didn't want to bring a baby into our relationship the
way it was. Charles continued to demand I do what he said,
including giving up my career. Again I refused. My job was
increasingly the only good thing in my life. And then...'

In the moments of silence that followed Polly felt the
tension building inside her, and could feel every rapid thud
of her heart against her ribs, not sure how to tell Luca the rest.

'And then?' he encouraged softly, his gentle understanding giving her the courage to go on.

'It was Halloween. I was six months pregnant. Charles
was waiting for me when I came home from work. He was
drunk, and there was a wildness in his eyes that scared me,'
she told him, her voice dropping to a hoarse whisper, her
body starting to shake. 'I'd hardly got inside the door when
he came for me. He was screaming abuse, and he was waving
a kitchen knife in his hand. I genuinely feared for my safety,
and that of my baby. He chased me out of the house. There
were people about, witnesses who later supported my version
of events. Scared, I tried to get away. I ran into the street and...

And,' she tried again, tears spilling from between her lashes, 'I was hit by a car.'

Luca swore long and hard in Italian, wrapping her in his arms and holding her close.

'I nearly died. My baby girl was already dead. The placental abruption and haemorrhaging were so bad that there was nothing else they could do. The only way to save my life was to do a hysterectomy—to take my baby and with her any chance I could ever have any more.'

'But you are alive. *Dio grazie.*'

'It didn't seem such a good deal in those early days. Charles came to the hospital, pretending to be a grieving husband, but then he went mad, accusing me of killing the baby and trying to attack me. Hospital Security restrained him and the police arrested him, the witness reports confirming what he had done on the day and, later, in the hospital. I was given protection and a restraining order stopping him coming near me. It all came out over the next weeks…his drinking, his addiction to poker on the internet, the vast amounts he had lost and now owed to various money-lenders, some more dodgy than others. He was clearly ill, and was committed for a time to a secure hospital. I was granted a divorce and chose to take my mother's maiden name. The house and everything we had went to settle Charles's debts. I had nothing—except of course, the money from Reg's house that Kate had persuaded me to hide away. As much as I didn't want to touch it, tainted as it was, it was all I had and helped me to survive the weeks of recuperation until I could go back to work. No at the same place. I couldn't face it, but I signed on for locum work while I decided what I wanted to do with my life.

'I hated London, felt insecure, as if I was looking over my shoulder, scared Charles might one day reappear. And there were the memories. So when Kate told me about the new job in Penhally, and persuaded me to return, it was like a new start, a new chapter.'

'You are amazing,' Luca whispered with admiration, nuzzling against her.

Polly shook her head. 'I'm not. I feel so guilty,' she confessed, tears sliding down her cheeks.

'What for?' Luca rested the palm of one hand over the physical scar that, four years on, was beginning to fade. The emotional ones still felt so raw. 'It was *not* your fault, *zingarella*.'

Polly sucked in a breath, scared Luca would hate her when he learned how selfish she had been. 'But I didn't intend to have children at all. When Charles tricked me and deliberately made me pregnant, at first I *didn't want the baby*. So when I lost her, it was as if I had made it happen, as if I had killed her, just like Charles said,' she sobbed.

Luca's hold tightened as he rolled them onto their sides, his free hand cupping her face and making her look at him. '*No!* No, Polly, you did *not* kill your baby. Charles attacked you, you had no option but to escape him. It was an accident, tragic and terrible, but an *accident*,' he insisted, nothing but understanding and compassion in his eyes.

'I didn't want her to die.'

'I know, *mio amore*.' He brushed a kiss across her forehead. 'And I'm so sorry for your pain. We will never forget your little girl. Had you given her a name?'

Polly nodded, her thoughts in turmoil. 'I was going to call her Yvonne Katherine, after my mother and Kate. And she would have been born a week or so after the twins were. I look at Rosie and Toni, and at other children the same age, and I wonder what my daughter might have been like now. I never wanted children, yet once I had become used to the knowledge I was going to have a baby, I loved her completely, and I yearned in a way I had never imagined to be a mother. Not only did I lose her, but I can never have another child.'

Luca was incredible…understanding, supportive, reverential of her lost baby, caring and gentle with her. He dried her eyes and made love to her with exquisite tenderness, telling her again and again that she was special and beautiful, just as he had done every day since.

She was almost coming to believe him. *Almost.* Self-doubt remained, locked deep inside. After checking the notes for the home visits she was about to make, she rose to her feet. A shiver rippled through her. Why did she have an impending sense of doom?

CHAPTER TEN

'YOUR relationship with Polly is serious, is it?'

Nick's voice came from Luca's consulting room and, as she neared the open door, Polly hesitated, her heart in her mouth as she waited for Luca's response.

'Polly is perfect. The twins love her.'

Luca's phone rang, masking Nick's next question. Polly edged forward, but when Luca spoke again, she halted, rooted to the spot in shock.

'I have no regrets, Nick. I've tried always to do what felt right,' he said, an edge of reserve behind the polite tone. 'And, yes, I plan to ask Polly to marry me—soon.'

Glad she had remained out of sight, Polly pressed a hand to her mouth to smother her gasp of shock. Luca was thinking permanence? With *her*? Cinderella didn't get to marry Prince Charming, not outside fairy-tales. The ghost of Plain Polly hadn't been fully exorcised.

'I appreciate that, Nick, but there's no going back.' She must have missed more of the men's conversation as Luca's statement puzzled her. Worse followed. 'I knew what I was doing when I made the decision. I'd make any sacrifice necessary to ensure my daughters' happiness.'

Polly stepped back from the doorway, Luca's words pounding in her head. Was that what being with her was to him…a sacrifice? The twins liked her and needed a woman's touch, so Luca would make do? All her insecurities returned to torment her. She would never be good enough. She was too plain and unattractive to capture the heart of a man like Luca. The message was loud and clear. By marrying her, by *sacrificing* himself, he was providing for his children. That's what mattered to him.

Tears stung Polly's eyes as she hurried towards the exit, unresponsive to those who greeted her, including Kate. She had to get out before she broke down completely. Because hearing Luca's words had made her realise how much she loved him. She'd fought against it, knowing he was dangerous, but in a very short time he had demolished her defences and stolen her heart. And he didn't want it. Not for himself. All he wanted was a mother for his children and, as much as she loved Rosie and Toni, she knew that would never be enough.

Frowning, Kate watched Polly rush out of the surgery. Something was wrong. The young woman had definitely been upset, but whatever could have happened? Concerned, and making a mental note to talk to Polly later, Kate headed for the stairs, just in time to encounter Nick as he left Luca's consulting room.

'Ah, Kate…' His smile was awkward, the tension that had simmered between them since her return to work seeming to increase by the day. 'A word, if you have a moment?'

Time alone with Nick was to be avoided, but at work it was impossible. 'All right.' Footsteps heavy with reluctance, she followed to his room.

'I was talking to Luca about his plans for the future,' he told her, closing the door and waving her to a chair.

Was that the cause of Polly's upset? Had she overheard

something bad enough to turn her face ashen and bring tears to her eyes? For now Kate tried to set Polly's situation aside, because she needed all her wits about her to maintain her guard with Nick.

'I'm hoping Luca and Polly will stay on and become junior partners in due time, as Oliver and Gabriel have done,' Nick continued. 'Things will become busier with the surgery expansion.'

Kate recognised the delaying tactic and wished he'd say why he'd wanted to speak with her. 'I'm sure the patients will appreciate the increased range of services.'

Having been involved in the practice since Nick and Marco Avanti had taken it over several years ago, Kate was proud of what had been achieved, and was excited for the future of the practice. It was a future in which she wanted to play a part but… She forced herself to look at Nick. Could she stay here if things between them failed to improve?

After everything that had happened, and all the times he had let her down and hurt her over Jem, why did her stupid heart still react to the sight and sound of him? Why was the right man wrong and the wrong man right? The question led her inexorably to Rob.

Dear Rob. He'd been wonderful to her throughout her ordeal, and he had embraced Jem, giving her son the male role model he so badly needed. She cared about Rob, deeply…but was that enough to sustain a permanent relationship? After their talk a few nights ago, she had three months to find an answer.

'I need to say this, Kate, so please hear me out,' Rob had begun, his voice unusually serious. 'I love you. I believe the four of us can be happy as a family unit. I know it's important for you not to make big decisions before seeing the oncologist in January, so I'm not going to ask before then,' he'd added, his smile endearing. 'But I want you to know I'd marry you tomorrow. My feelings and desire to be with you aren't dependent on the result. No...' He'd cupped her face, pressing one thumb to her lips. 'Please, don't say anything—just don't close your mind to the kind of life we could have.'

Kate had thought of Rob's words often in the last days. How could she not? Rob was a generous, giving and loving man who offered her and Jem stability and happiness. Accepting his proposal, when it came, would be the sensible and obvious thing to do. But—

'How are you getting on back at work, Kate?' Nick asked, redirecting her attention.

'I'm enjoying it,' she told him honestly. 'It's been a long time.'

He shifted, anxious and ill at ease. 'We've missed you. *I've* missed you,' he added, shocking her as much by the intimate tone of his voice as the words themselves.

'Nick—'

'I've had time to think these last months,' he continued, forestalling her protest. 'I've behaved badly to you and Jeremiah. I'm not excusing it, but finding out the truth was a shock, one I've yet to come to terms with.' He leaned forward, resting folded arms on the desk, the expression in his eyes sincere. 'We've been through a great deal you and I. I not only value you as a colleague, one who's been loyal and hardworking from the first, but also as a close friend and confidante.'

Tears stung her eyes. 'Thank you. I don't know what to say,' she murmured, unnerved by the electric atmosphere growing in the room.

'I want things to be different between us, Kate.'

'Different, how?' A mix of emotions welled within her, ranging from panic and confusion to hope and shock.

Nick's brow knotted in concentration. 'I regret the distance that's grown between us, the awkwardness and loss of friendship. And, yes,' he added, with a rare admission of his own failings, 'I've been responsible for that. But I *have* missed you, and I've hated being on the sidelines while you've been through your operation and treatment, worrying about you and wanting to be with you, to help.'

Again his words shocked her. Part of her wanted to remind him that *he* was the one who had distanced himself, who had made no effort whatsoever, and who had let her down when she'd asked for his reassurance about Jem's security should something happen during her operation, or afterwards. It had been Rob who had stepped up to the plate and shouldered everything. But what good would it do to rub that in now? Nick *was* making an effort, and it was what she had wanted for the last eighteen months, since Jem's real paternity had been made known to him.

'You and Rob…' Nick cleared his throat, lids lowering to shadow the expression in his eyes. 'Do you love him?'

'I'd say it wasn't your business, but I suppose it is, in part, because of how things may affect Jem. We have mentioned the possibility of marriage at some point, if that's what you want to know,' she told him, knowing she was embellishing the truth but watching him carefully to assess his reaction.

Sitting back in his chair, he steepled his hands under his chin, his gaze direct as he faced her, his tension and displeasure evident. 'I see. And do you think that's the best thing to do?'

'The best for whom? Me…or Jem?' she parried, hope turning to disappointment as she guessed the possible direction this was going. 'Rob treats Jem just the same as his own son, they've bonded well and Jem has really benefited from having a male influence in his life, not to mention the emotional support while I was ill.'

'I see,' Nick repeated, a muscle pulsing along his jaw. 'So there's no hope for us?'

'What sort of an "us" did you have in mind, Nick?' she enquired, her heart thudding as her tension and annoyance increased.

Looking uncomfortable, Nick sighed. 'I don't know. As I said, I miss you in my life in so many ways. I'd like us to regain what was lost—maybe to take things further.'

'And Jem? Where does he fit in?'

Pain lanced inside her as she read the answer in his eyes. Damn the man for doing this! And damn her heart for still wanting him, clinging to a hope and love that seemed as impossible now as it always had done. Anger and disappointment drove her to her feet.

'You're no closer to acknowledging Jem, are you? This isn't about us at all, is it, Nick? Your world has been rattled, I'm not there as I used to be, uncomplaining and reliable. You don't love me, I don't think you even *want* me. You just don't want someone else to have me or to have to watch as another man earns the love and respect and trust of a son you cannot bear to admit is yours.'

'Kate, please,' he appealed, also rising to his feet.

'No, Nick. We've been over this endlessly. You'll never accept Jem. You use your own children as an excuse,' she accused, moving towards the door and raising her chin in defiance. 'You're so busy worrying what Jack, Lucy and Edward might think of the fact that Jem was conceived that fateful night of the storm while their mother was still alive. But has it never occurred to you what they'll think now, when the truth comes out?' she demanded, one hand clinging to the doorhandle for much-needed support, her whole body shaking. 'And the truth *will* be known one day, Nick, as Jem grows older and the similarities between you become more obvious, people are going to notice and speculate. Your adult children are all wonderful, caring, decent people. How are they going to feel when they discover how you've shunned Jem and refused to accept him as your son?'

Kate made herself face him, seeing the anger, surprise and

the touch of fear he couldn't hide. They were as far apart as ever and she hated that it hurt it so much. Unable to bear any more, she opened the door, praying for him to stop her but knowing he wouldn't. She closed it quietly behind her, leaving Nick to struggle with his demons while she tried, for the umpteenth time, to put the pieces of her heart back together.

Taking a deep breath, she squared her shoulders and raised her chin. She wasn't going to let Nick do this to her any more and she had other people to think of rather than herself. With that in mind, an image of Polly's tear-stained face returned to her, and she went in search of Luca—her own life might be far from settled, but at least she could hope for a happy ending for the young couple so precious to her.

A mix of relief, fear and confusion slammed in Luca's chest as he took the stairs two at a time and discovered Polly sitting on the bedroom floor, Jasper the puppy in her arms as she rocked back and forth, the evidence of tear-tracks on her pale cheeks. Thank God for Kate…again. When she'd popped into his consulting room earlier in the afternoon to tip him off about Polly's distress, he'd been desperate to go after her, but he'd had to wait until he'd finished his list, careful to not let his own worries affect the care he gave his patients.

And now he was here. And so was Polly. Thankfully, the twins were at a birthday party at the vicarage, which meant there was time alone to talk. He needed to find out what was wrong and, if Kate was correct, what snippet of his conversation with Nick Polly had overheard and had taken exception to. She looked up as he walked into the room and he managed a shaky smile.

'Hello, *zingarella*.' Although he wanted nothing more that to sweep her into his arms and make love to her, he sat on the edge of the bed, as close to her as possible, and prayed that whatever had gone wrong could be put right.

'Hi.'

Scared of doing or saying the wrong thing, Luca felt tense. 'What happened, *mio amore*? Something you overheard upset you?'

'Yes,' she whispered.

Unable to bear even this distance between them, Luca took a chance and slipped to his knees on the floor, edging closer and taking one of her hands in his. 'We made an agreement to always tell each other the truth, no matter what. I'll always be honest with you, Polly. Please, tell me what's wrong.'

'I can't be what you want me to be,' she finally said, confusing him even more.

'I don't understand.' He shook his head in puzzlement. 'I don't want you to be anything but yourself. You're perfect as you are.'

'As a mother for your children.'

The way she flung the words at him took him by surprise. 'I come as a package deal, you know that. I thought you liked the girls, were bonding with them.'

'I do. I am. But…' She broke off. 'It's not enough,' she continued, almost stopping his heart.

'Not enough?' Instinctively, he drew her hand towards him and held it over his rapidly beating heart. He swallowed, then forced himself to say the words. 'You do not care something for me also? You cannot find a way to come to love me, too?'

She was staring at him as if he had grown two heads. 'What are you talking about?'

'You said caring about the children was not enough.'

'It isn't,' she repeated, hurting him anew. 'Not long term. You told Nick you'd make any sacrifice for your daughters…like marrying me to give them a mother. I thought it was you who was just making do, who couldn't come to love or care for me.' Luca's mouth dropped open in shock, but she continued before he could correct her. 'I know I'm nothing like Elaine. She was beautiful and feminine. And I have nothing else to offer. I can't even give you children.'

As the words finished on a sob, Luca carefully removed Jasper from her lap, then pulled her into his arms, wanting to laugh and cry at one and the same time, angry and relieved all at once.

'No, no, no, you have it all wrong, *amore mio,*' he chided. 'How can you think that of me? Had I just wanted any woman as a mother for the girls, why would I have waited four years? I hadn't wanted anyone in my life, hadn't noticed another woman existed until the moment I stepped into your consulting room that first morning. Just looking at you was enough to bring me rushing out of hibernation. You brought me back to life, *zingarella,* a life I was living only for the twins. I didn't think I could ever have anything for myself again, that I would ever feel or hope or dream or love. You've given all that back to me, Polly. You brought light into the darkness. That the twins love you, too, is a bonus, but I would still want to spend the rest of my life with you even if I'd never had the twins. You made me realise there *was* a life for me, one I wanted to live again if I could share it with you.'

Tears squeezed between Polly's lashes and trickled down her cheeks. She pressed a hand to her mouth to stop another sob escaping. Dear God, Luca meant it. He really meant every word he had said. She just had to believe, to allow herself to trust again—herself and him. Either she could stay alone, scared to reach out for what she most wanted, frightened to take another risk, or she could reach for her own dreams and embrace everything Luca was offering.

She'd left the surgery with every intention of packing her things and going back to the flat in Bridge Street. Her final house call had been to Gertrude Stanbury who, as ever, missed nothing and had demanded an explanation. By the time Polly had finished a tearful and somewhat disjointed account, her former headmistress had subjected her to the full force of her uncompromising grey gaze.

'Are you sure you are not looking for an excuse?'

'What do you mean?' Polly had asked, taken aback by the accusation.

'It is easier to blame something or someone else, to use that to back away, rather than to take the risk of being hurt again, of having to take responsibility for trusting your own judgement.'

Polly had wanted to deny the truth of the words.

'I've always admired your inner strength and your courage. Don't let them fail you now. You have another chance for real happiness, Polly—you mustn't be afraid to take it. That kind of love doesn't come around every day, so grasp it with both hands because you never know if and when you will get another chance.'

'But—'

'What if…two saddest words in the English language. Don't make the mistakes I did, Polly. You have so much courage. And no one deserves happiness more than you do. If you love Luca as much as I think you do, don't run off in the heat of the moment. Give him a chance to explain and find out the truth first. Follow your heart.'

Polly had returned to Keeper's Cottage with Ms Stanbury's words ringing in her ears and knowing she had two choices. Run away or wait for Luca. She'd imagined life without Luca and the girls and there had been no decision to make. And so she sat on the floor in the bedroom, Jasper's warm little body snuggled in her arms, fighting the inner demons that told her she wasn't good enough for a man like Luca, that Plain Polly from Penhally wasn't lovable.

And the gamble had been worth taking because Luca had

come home and had laid his heart on the line. For her. Luca had lost Elaine and he was brave enough to try again, knowing life was uncertain. Whether she had one day, one year or a whole lifetime, she wanted to spend it all loving him. This, oh, so special man who made her feel, for the first time in her life, that maybe she was worth something and maybe she deserved to be happy and loved. It was a miracle in itself. And he had another miracle gift to give her, too. Having thought she had lost the chance of ever knowing the joy of mother-hood, Luca was prepared to give her a precious gift…that of being a mother to his beautiful children.

'I love you so much, Luca,' she sobbed, and the naked happiness and relief in his deep brown eyes showed her what those words meant to him. 'I didn't believe I was worth loving.'

'I will prove to you every day just how much you are loved,' he vowed.

'I love you. I love Rosie and Toni…and I love Jasper.' She giggled as the mischievous puppy tried to push his way between them, stubby tail wagging happily.

If she had a tail, it would be wagging, too! She hadn't believed she could be this happy, could have so much in her life. Wrapping her arms around Luca's neck, she sank into his embrace, feeling safe for the first time, as if she had finally found her real home, the place she belonged. Penhally had brought her pain in the past but she had returned here to face it—in doing so she had found her future, one filled with love—with her sexy Italian and his adorable twins.

EPILOGUE

THE late January day was cold but a weak sun hung low in a pale blue sky sprinkled with off-white clouds. Most of the month had been wet and windy. Surely today's break in the weather was a good omen?

It was one of the happiest days of her life, Kate reflected, giving away her beloved goddaughter, who had known so much heartache in her young life, and watching her marry the man of her dreams in a simple but beautifully poignant ceremony in Penhally's small church.

Polly looked ethereal and beautiful, glowing with happiness as she and Luca pledged their vows to love, honour and cherish each other. And it was clear to all that they did. The handsome Italian with the loving, giving heart had worked a miracle, helping Polly to set her unhappy past behind her and sharing with her the hope and expectation for the future. A future that included Luca's most special gift—his twin girls. A gift of motherhood for Polly, something the young woman had never expected to know after the tragic loss of her unborn daughter.

'Don't they look adorable?' Chloe whispered.

Kate turned her head to smile at her friend and colleague beside her. 'They are as cute as anything!' Kate agreed.

She and Chloe turned as one to watch Rosie and Toni perform their roles as flower girls and ring bearers, the beaming smiles on their faces a testament to their delight at having Polly as their new mother. Today was definitely a day for joy and celebration.

Yesterday had been, too. Kate had yet to fully grasp the relief that had swamped her when Dr Bowers, her oncologist, had told her that the cancer *had* gone. No one knew what the future held, but for now, at least, her own was brighter and fuller. But not uncomplicated, she allowed, all too conscious of Rob sitting on her other side.

Any day Rob might ask her to marry him and, despite all her thinking, she was no closer to an answer. Her gaze strayed across the narrow aisle to Nick. The wrong man in so many ways and yet, despite all that had passed between them and all the pain he had caused her, still the man that her stupid heart yearned for. Unless Nick could acknowledge and embrace Jem wholeheartedly, there could be no future for them. And she couldn't wait for ever for that miracle to happen.

Kate dragged her gaze from the man who had, over the years, been friend, confidant, boss, colleague and one-night lover, refocusing her gaze on Polly, determined to put thoughts of her own future aside while she celebrated her god-daughter's special day.

'I can now declare you husband and wife,' Rev Saunders announced with a smile. 'You may kiss your bride.'

Polly turned to Luca, seeing the love in his eyes. Their gazes locked. Their mouths met. And they sealed their bond. The fingers of one hand were linked with his, while the fingers of her other held a tiny one belonging to Rosie. And with Toni's held by her father, the four of them were united as a family.

As they walked together down the aisle, Polly had a lump in her throat as she met and returned the smiles of those who had gathered to celebrate this day with them. Kate, who had done so much for her all her life and who had made this day all the better with two treasured gifts…the news that she was cancer free, and an album filled with copies of photographs she had unearthed in her attic of the mother Polly had loved and lost and had never expected to visualise again.

Jane and Brian Watson, though frail, had been determined to attend and give their blessing. Their generosity in accepting her role in the lives of Luca and their granddaughters made Polly's heart swell with gratitude. She could assure them that Elaine would never be forgotten, having given life to the twins at the expense of her own.

Nick was there, an excellent doctor and a good boss, but a man who needed to make peace with himself. Gertrude Stanbury's presence brought another smile to Polly's face. She owed her old headmistress a great deal, not just for her help when she'd been young but for her advice last autumn not to be afraid to take risks again. Next came Georgie and her husband Luka, the couple becoming good friends these last months, as well as satisfying the twins' enthusiasm for all things pony!

The rest of the places were filled by colleagues who had become good friends and who did much to make Penhally the special place it was…Oliver and Chloe, Gabriel and Lauren, Dragan and Melinda, and Sam and Gemma, herself expecting their first baby in March. Even Charlotte and James had come, bonded through voluntary work with Charlotte's rape crisis centre—and by puppies!

Polly felt as if she was floating on a cloud of happiness. She was scarcely aware of the photographs being taken and she couldn't remember who she'd spoken to. All she was aware of was Luca, and she welcomed the few moments they were able to be alone as everyone travelled up the hill to

Smuggler's for a buffet lunch, one that included a sinfully gorgeous white chocolate and raspberry cake. It was a sign of how far she had come in dealing with her food issues, thanks to Luca, that Polly intended to eat a huge piece of that cake in public and enjoy every moment of it!

'Happy?' Luca asked as they lingered a moment before getting out of the car.

'Not really,' she murmured, feeling guilty for teasing him when she saw the panic and hurt in his deep brown eyes. 'Happy doesn't even begin to cover the extent of my euphoria!'

She giggled as his fingers cupped her chin, the sexy, smouldering expression on his face fanning the fires of desire that constantly burned within her. 'Oh, you're in so much trouble now, *zingarella*,' he warned her, the husky rumble of his voice sending a delicious shiver down her spine.

'I do hope so! And, Luca, you never did tell me what *zingarella* means,' she reminded him with a mock pout. 'Surely today of all days…'

His slow-burn smile brought a dimple to his cheek and made her warm all over. 'It came to me as soon as I met you, with your unique style of clothes. Just one of the many, many things I love about you, little gypsy,' he whispered, his fingers stroking her cheek before he leaned in for an all-too-short but passionate kiss.

A knock on the car window ended their brief moment alone and despite planning it and looking forward to it, Polly now wished they could skip the buffet entirely.

'It will soon be over,' Luca murmured in her ear, accurately guessing the direction of her thoughts. 'And anticipation heightens the pleasure, no?' he added with a naughty smile. 'Do not worry, *mio amore*, I will make the wait worth your while.'

As if such a promise was going to achieve anything but

raise her pulse and her blood pressure and make her even more impatient!

Rosie and Toni stayed close to them through the buffet, and Polly once more gave thanks for the gift Luca had given her, sharing with her these precious children. At times she still grieved for her own lost daughter, but Luca's understanding eased the ache. And to prove to her that Yvonne Katherine would never be forgotten as a much-missed part of their family, he'd taken her completely by surprise by having the names tattooed under those of the twins' over his heart. The gesture had made her cry, and had provided yet more evidence of how special this man was.

It felt hours later before things began to wind down. The twins were staying with Kate, Rob, the boys and puppies Bruno and Jasper. So much a part of them, it had been a difficult decision, but they'd ruled out a full honeymoon and so wanted this one weekend alone to savour the reality of their marriage.

And now it was time to go. Polly looked round and saw the twins approaching their father, hands fisting in the material of his trousers to claim his attention. Smiling, he hunkered down to meet them face to face, listening as they whispered to him in Italian. Polly heard the words but couldn't understand what they were saying. Her breath stuttered as Luca looked up and caught her gaze, allowing her to see the moisture filming his eyes. He returned his attention to the girls and, nodding his head, he gave them a gentle nudge towards her.

Rosie and Toni approached her where she sat, stuffed on cake and dazed with happiness. 'Hello, darlings,' she greeted them as they arrived one on either side of her. 'You look so beautiful and never have there been better flower girls or ring bearers,' she praised, earning huge grins.

'We want to ask you something,' Rosie said, reaching out

to hold Toni's hand. 'Today's special, isn't it? We really become a proper family?'

'That's right.' Polly's throat felt tight with emotion.

'Well…'

Rosie hesitated and Toni frowned. 'Go *on*, Rosie. Papà said to ask her.'

'OK.'

Polly looked down into two pairs of brown eyes, so like their father's. 'What is it?'

'Toni and me want…' Rosie began, clearly nervous, so Polly didn't correct her grammar. 'Please can we call you Mummy?'

Their faces swam before her as her eyes filled with tears. Speechless, fearing her heart would burst, Polly gathered them to her and hugged them tight. 'Yes, darlings, if you want to, I'd be very happy,' she finally managed, her voice choked with emotion.

'We definitely want to,' Toni asserted, pressing a kiss to her cheek.

Rosie kissed her other cheek. 'We love you, Mummy Polly.'

'I love you, too. Both of you. So very much.'

Polly stood with them still in her arms as Luca joined them, his arms wrapping around them and binding them as a family. Somehow, Plain Polly from Penhally had fought off the darkness and had emerged into the light. She wanted to pinch herself to make sure this dream was true, but she had her hands full—full of love and hope and joy in the shape of the Italian husband she adored and the twins she would be proud to mother. The four of them together…a family for ever.

MEDICAL™ 2-in-1

Coming next month

EMERGENCY: PARENTS NEEDED
by Jessica Matthews

Paramedic Joe finds himself caring for a baby daughter he never knew existed, but what does a bachelor know about babies? Bubbly colleague Maggie must make this sinfully handsome man realise he *can* be a good father... and husband!

A BABY TO CARE FOR
by Lucy Clark

Orphaned newborn baby – stand-in mum needed: how can Outback paediatrician Iris refuse? Especially when local playboy Dr Dex Crawford offers to help! Falling for both man and baby, Iris hopes their temporary family can become full-time bliss...

PLAYBOY SURGEON, TOP-NOTCH DAD
by Janice Lynn

Single mum Blair guards her heart fiercely – especially against notorious playboys like her new boss, Dr Oz Manning. But might this beautiful nurse and her adorable little girl be the ones to turn this lovable rogue into a family man for ever...?

ONE SUMMER IN SANTA FE
by Molly Evans

Devoted to his patients, Taylor has managed to avoid emotional involvement, until he's blown away by his new temporary nurse. This dynamic doctor has one short summer to convince her to stay with him, permanently!

On sale 5th February 2010

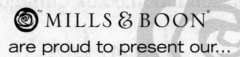

MILLS & BOON

are proud to present our...

Book of the Month

An Officer
and a Millionaire
by Maureen Child
from Mills & Boon®
Desire™ 2-in-1

The broad-shouldered military man had no
patience with games. Margie had to go. She'd
been masquerading as his spouse and living in his
house. Now all his skills were focused on payback:
he'd have that "wedding night"!

Enjoy double the romance in this
great-value 2-in-1!
An Officer and a Millionaire by Maureen Child and
Mr Strictly Business by Day Leclaire

Mills & Boon® Desire™ 2-in-1
Available 18th December 2009

*Something to say about our
Book of the Month?
Tell us what you think!
millsandboon.co.uk/community*

millsandboon.co.uk Community

Join Us!

The Community is the perfect place to meet and chat to kindred spirits who love books and reading as much as you do, but it's also the place to:

- ■ Get the inside scoop from authors about their latest books
- ■ Learn how to write a romance book with advice from our editors
- ■ Help us to continue publishing the best in women's fiction
- ■ Share your thoughts on the books we publish
- ■ Befriend other users

Forums: Interact with each other as well as authors, editors and a whole host of other users worldwide.

Blogs: Every registered community member has their own blog to tell the world what they're up to and what's on their mind.

Book Challenge: We're aiming to read 5,000 books and have joined forces with The Reading Agency in our inaugural Book Challenge.

Profile Page: Showcase yourself and keep a record of your recent community activity.

Social Networking: We've added buttons at the end of every post to share via digg, Facebook, Google, Yahoo, technorati and de.licio.us.

www.millsandboon.co.uk

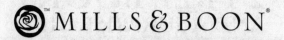

2 FREE BOOKS
AND A SURPRISE GIFT

We would like to take this opportunity to thank you for reading this Mills & Boon® book by offering you the chance to take TWO more specially selected books from the Medical™ series absolutely FREE! We're also making this offer to introduce you to the benefits of the Mills & Boon® Book Club™—

- **FREE home delivery**
- **FREE gifts and competitions**
- **FREE monthly Newsletter**
- **Exclusive Mills & Boon Book Club offers**
- **Books available before they're in the shops**

Accepting these FREE books and gift places you under no obligation to buy, you may cancel at any time, even after receiving your free books. Simply complete your details below and return the entire page to the address below. You don't even need a stamp!

YES Please send me 2 free Medical books and a surprise gift. I understand that unless you hear from me, I will receive 5 superb new stories every month including two 2-in-1 books priced at £4.99 each and a single book priced at £3.19, postage and packing free. I am under no obligation to purchase any books and may cancel my subscription at any time. The free books and gift will be mine to keep in any case.

Ms/Mrs/Miss/Mr _____ Initials _____

Surname _____

Address _____

_____ Postcode _____

Send this whole page to: Mills & Boon Book Club, Free Book Offer, FREEPOST NAT 10298, Richmond, TW9 1BR